Yvonne Finnegan has been a Jane Austen fan since the age of 15. She grew up in a small community of French-speaking expatriates in Washington, D.C., where she attended the French International School (Lycée Rochambeau) and Georgetown University. Now living in New Mexico, she spends her days hiking, reading, writing, and traveling to long-distance running destinations.

This novel is dedicated to my three amazing children, Mark, Alix, and Natasha, and my adorable grandchildren, Noémi and Corbin.

Yvonne Finnegan

THE PEMBERLEY PAPERS

AUSTIN MACAULEY PUBLISHERS™

LONDON • CAMBRIDGE • NEW YORK • SHARJAH

Austin Macauley is committed to publishing works of quality and integrity. In this spirit, we are proud to offer this book to our readers; however, the story, the experiences, and the words are the author's alone.

Ordering Information
Quantity sales: special discounts are available on quantity purchases by corporations, associations, and others. For details, contact the publisher at the address below.

Publisher's Cataloging-in-Publication data
Finnegan, Yvonne
The Pemberley Papers

ISBN 9781645369752 (Paperback)
ISBN 9781645369769 (Hardback)
ISBN 9781645369783 (ePub e-book)

Library of Congress Control Number: 2020909907

www.austinmacauley.com/us

First Published (2020)
Austin Macauley Publishers LLC
40 Wall Street, 28th Floor
New York, NY 10005
USA

mail-usa@austinmacauley.com
+1 (646) 5125767

Many thanks to Alix and Natasha, who read the raw manuscript and pronounced it entertaining. Your enthusiasm means the world to me. This work would not have seen the light of day without the Albuquerque chapter of NaNoWriMo (National Novel Writing Month), whose encouraging members spurred me to get this writing done (well, most of it) within the 30 days of November 2017. Thank you also to John Bell for his sense of humor and daily doses of morale-boosting.

"[*Pride and Prejudice*] is rather too light, and bright, and sparkling; it wants shade…" Letter of Jane Austen to Cassandra Austen, 4 February 1813. *In Jane Austen's Letters to her Sister Cassandra and Others*, ed. R. W. Chapman, 2nd ed., p. 299. London: Oxford University Press, 1952.

"'[Mr. Darcy and Mr. Wickham] have both been deceived, I dare say, in some way or other, of which we can form no idea. […] It is, in short, impossible for us to conjecture the causes or circumstances which may have alienated them, without actual blame on either side.'" Jane Bennet to Elizabeth Bennet, chapter XVII, P. 85, *In the Oxford Illustrated Jane Austen, vol. II, 3rd ed., Pride and Prejudice*, ed. R. W. Chapman. London: Oxford University Press, 1932.

PART I

Gulliver

Pemberley, Derbyshire, August 28

My life is over. Master Willy is not coming back. It's my fault.

Well, no. Not entirely my fault. Perhaps I WAS in the wrong, but I was only trying to be friendly.

Miss Georgie never has any objections to my pawing and sniffing. She laughs when I put my paws on her shoulders. But *this* girl—I should have known! That mushroom scent! Hint of vinegar and putrid duck! Ill omen. Mushroom girl shrieked at my ritual of welcome. She kicked me in the belly. I snapped. I bit, but just a little.

She screamed. Master Willy stared at me. Perplexity and horror combined. "Gulliver! NO!"

What an uproar! Mushroom girl peeled away. Faked limp (I am not a dupe of these things). Master Willy ran after her. I was taken to the stables (oh indignity) by Horse Boy Harry. They leashed me like a beast of burden and left me there for hours. They forgot to feed me, too.

Now the house is almost deserted. Mushroom girl and her sister left. Master Willy left. Mr. Charles left. Mrs. Reynolds came to liberate me, gave me a bone with plenty of meat on it. Patted me on the head, and said, "Not to worry, Gully, me little lad, not to worry." I chewed on the bone, only to please her. Really, I was not hungry by then.

My life is over. I will lie here and just die. He is angry with me and will never come back.

September 1

O blessed, blessed day! Master Willy is back, and he does not hate me. In fact, the opposite. He was happy to see me. "Good dog, good dog, good dog!" And then, those cryptic words, "Gully, old boy, I believe you saved me from a very inconvenient situation." I am not sure what that means. The cloud on him is gone, not a whiff of it left. Whatever can that mean? But oh, I love that sweet scratching behind the ears, and that low rumbling voice. He loves me again. He is the best.

September 4

Aaahh! Something about early fall. Formidable scents, numerous and undulating, cool breezes wafting. I go mad with glee. Master Willy is happy to be back and loves me again, he does. We take long walks, sometimes we run. I love to run.

I heard them talk in the kitchen: mushroom girl is not coming back. Life is wonderful.

Fitzwilliam Darcy

Pemberley, Derbyshire, September 18

What a fool Charles is. I shall never understand how he can be so precipitous—bordering on flighty—in making momentous decisions. Unheeding of my advice to purchase the Hatsworth estate, which was well within his power to acquire, and which would have made us neighbors of sorts—a mere 70 miles from Pemberley—he has quite inconceivably signed his agreement upon an estate in the South, in Hertfordshire, a property that was to let, not to purchase.

Caroline was not kind in her rebukes this evening, and Louisa was scarcely more civil. Indeed, they are impatient for him to be truly settled now that he has been of age two years already, and they would prefer a more Northern exposure, as it were. The conversation went something like this:

"How could you make such a decision on a whim?" said Louisa in that whiny, exasperated tone of hers.

"Not a whim," Bingley protested. "The property was highly recommended by the curate of North Lambton, whose cousin—"

"Charles, that is not the issue. Why did you not consult us?" Caroline cut in.

"But… The truth is… It has a splendid library that…"

"Hah! For all the time *you* ever spend with a book! One might think you perfectly illiterate!" Caroline said. Her sneering tone annoyed me. 'Tis true that Charles is not the most well-read fellow I ever met, but it was inappropriate of her to upbraid him so, especially in company. Georgiana looked up in astonishment from her work. I had to intervene.

I clapped my book shut, started up from my chair, and championed Charles's cause in the most ardent tones, praised the charms of the southern countryside in the fall, and declared myself ready to accompany him when he takes possession at Michaelmas. That nailed the sisters' beaks shut. They looked quite chastened. I rarely express myself so vehemently. Blessed silence followed, broken only by the fire crackling in the hearth. I was gratified by

Georgiana's almost imperceptible smile, as I was by Charles's grateful expression. Hurst continued snoring unperturbed.

So, to this Netherfield estate shall I go. Bingley is not to be left on his own in uncharted waters, and he needs my helping hand. I do hope this impulsive decision will not prove as disagreeably consequential as his last few ideas. After all, it was due to his bumbling excess of nicety that we found ourselves embroiled with the Edwards sisters. That, fortunately, is history. Thanks to Gulliver. Good little fellow! As a reward, I shall bring him along in my southerly saunter.

Netherfield, Hertfordshire, October 3

I suppose Charles can be half forgiven for allowing his inclinations to supersede his reason. Netherfield is a pleasant property, quite suitable for his station in life. At this time of year, the woods are entering autumn glory. Cool nights provide excellent sleeping conditions, and the afternoons are warm and golden.

Today, Bingley is busy flitting to and fro, visiting his new neighbors. The sisters are not expected here for another few days. I savor the solitude, unhampered by shrill female voices. Just the thing for long strolls with Gully. Poor lad! He seemed quite despondent and thin when I returned from London after delivering the injured Miss Edwards back to her indignant family. Mrs. Reynolds said he ate next to nothing while I was gone. But he looks better already. Loyal Gully! Little does he know what I owe him—the bite that saved! I could hardly keep a steadfast countenance when Miss Edwards declared, as we parted, that any engagement between us was now quite impossible, seeing that I had been lacking in respect by not immediately putting the ferocious animal down. Apparently, she was deeply offended by my tepid apologies. Well, so be it.

As if she had been hurt! He barely snapped; no blood was drawn.

As if an engagement had ever been envisaged... I was speechless with astonishment. Where the devil did she see an engagement looming?

I have difficulty comprehending females sometimes, and I feel as though I have narrowly escaped a most harrowing situation. Again, it has been hammered into my brain that it is very dangerous to pay attention to any woman, no matter how enticing her smiles may be, how nonchalant her demeanor, before one has thoroughly studied her character. It seems they are always scheming. I must be less naïve from now on and remain on my guard.

Netherfield, October 6

Bingley informed me that an Assembly is planned in Meryton, a village just a few miles from here, in a se'enight. He has secured invitations for all of us from a local knighted tradesman named Lucas. *SIR WILLIAM* Lucas. A ponderous, exclamatory fellow who has already returned Bingley's visit (twice) and regaled us with interminable tales of his presentation at Court. Caroline, Louisa, and Hurst are due to arrive tomorrow.

Bingley's social energies are remarkable. He has already met with a good number of the landed gentry here. I do not relish the thought of a country assembly, where more ladies of the ilk of Miss Edwards—except in a low, rustic incarnation—are bound to be present, ready to ensnare. But I must brace myself for the inevitable. In a more positive light, I am hopeful that a suitor might be found for Caroline among the young men here. Although her supercilious airs may frighten away the local lads, her 20,000 pounds may render her society—and an alliance—supportable to some, just as Louisa's share secured Mr. Hurst. It would make Bingley's life infinitely more pleasant to have her settled. And, I daresay, mine as well.

In the meantime, I am enjoying the perusal of the Netherfield library. Clearly the owner is a man of taste and education; besides the English and Classical authors, there is a tolerable collection of French and Italian works, a few of which I do not have at Pemberley and must make a point to purchase; although Voltaire and Montesquieu may be out of favor among my countrymen—out of excessive patriotism perhaps—they do make for provocative reading; in fact, much wisdom is to be found, in my opinion, in any work that a reputable printer finds fit to print—if only to sharpen one's wits in formulating disagreements with an erroneous point of view.

Even novels have value (although I discourage Georgiana from reading any), especially if one reads them with a critical stance. I use literature of all kinds to hone my ability to see things clearly, rationally, and with unprejudiced eyes.

I find it curious that not one of Charles's five sisters is ever to be seen with a book in hand. I have made it a point that Georgiana will not be left ignorant, as so many girls seem to be. They are merely asked to learn the Kings and Queens of England and a few phrases of French, and then their brains are left to wither away. I have instructed Mrs. Annesley to have Georgiana diligently follow the program of study that I drew up before I left.

I took a rather stern approach with Georgiana myself in that regard upon saying goodbye, but she disarmed me with her playful embrace. She declared that she would do exactly as she pleased in my absence but that since nothing pleased her better than pleasing me, I would not be disappointed, and I could quiz her as much as I liked upon my return. Sometimes she surprises me with such declarations that are half-impertinent, half-adoring. She is so young. When I think how close I came to losing her…

October 8

Caroline and Mr. and Mrs. Hurst and their retinue of servants arrived as a pouring rain was darkening the lanes. Complaints rained just as hard inside, immediately and incessantly. How backward the country, how rutted and muddy the roads, how inconvenient the inn, how dirty the carriage, how disgusting the sustenance proffered along the way, etc. They declared, with reproachful looks in my direction, that they had left Georgiana inconsolable at not being allowed to come to Netherfield to join our party. But after what happened, I believe it is safest to keep Georgiana out of society for a while, and I stolidly ignored their jagged arrows. I find that silence is a most efficacious response to impertinence.

October 10

We are settling into a routine. Charles and I comb the countryside on horseback every day that is fine—and many have been fine since we have been here. The sisters stay at home, carp and cavil, receive visitors with mellifluous tones, mock them once they have left, play the pianoforte and sing duets (rather shrilly), and work their endless embroideries. Caroline sighs often, remarking that Pemberley is infinitely superior to this place and hoping that Charles will soon be done indulging his Netherfield folly, as she calls it. He ignores her speeches, with a serene countenance. I admit she tries my patience. Were she my sister (God forbid!), I would not allow such sharp discourse. Mr. Hurst revives himself from his numerous naps only to bully us into playing *vingt et un* or whist in the evening and to drink himself into oblivion once again.

While this life may be perfectly acceptable for a few weeks, and although Bingley finds great pleasure in entertaining new acquaintances and returning their visits, I try to avoid this tedious social intercourse and find myself absent from the house much of the day. Gully is a lifesaver in this respect, and I always feel better after a long walk. But I daresay I shall go mad in a fortnight unless something happens to relieve the monotony.

Sometimes I wish I could be more like Charles and find amusement and joy in society. I wish I had his ease of repartee and that ingenuous, endearing tone of voice that many, including myself, find so charming. But it seems I am constrained by my character, and all the good will in the world will not turn me into a social butterfly. Perhaps I should go to Town soon nonetheless, and bring Georgiana, for her skills on the pianoforte have improved to the point that her current teacher has declared himself quite outdone by his pupil.

That accursed Assembly! It has been threatening like a tempest on the horizon for a week, and now it is upon us. Bingley is looking forward to it with the enthusiasm of a little boy who has been promised sweets, for there is talk of a few local beauties; and the sisters are outdoing themselves in their contemptuous predictions of the savagery we are about to witness. I do not know which of these two attitudes is most to be pitied. I confess I may agree more with the sisters than with Charles. But I am tired of their platitudes and affectations—what Louisa would call *sournoiseries* in other women—and so I plan to remove myself as much as possible from their society today. Long walks in the woods of Netherfield these next few days may do the trick. Gulliver needs exercise. I am happy to have brought him.

Gulliver

Netherfield, October 11

Delightful, enchanting! Master Willy is truly my best friend. We have been going out and traipsing the countryside every day, for hours, just he and I. I am no longer a puppy; I can go all day. Master Willy gives me leisure to sniff about and explore, and I can tell you that these woods are at least as delicious as those of Pemberley—a true fairyland. Brooks, ferns, squirrels, snakes, frogs, moles and voles galore. I almost caught a duck today.

Nothing is better than coming home after those long rambles, filling my belly with a most convivial mush, and lying before the hearth.

There is something about Master Willy, though. It has happened before. It is happening again. He looks happy to go out but anxious about something. Unsettled. I hope it has nothing to do with that mushroom girl. Tonight, he is sipping a glass of wine, staring intently at the fire. Then he will start up and walk about as in a fit. Then he sits down again.

Well, time to nap.

October 14

Something very strange has happened to Master Willy! Last night he went out with the rest of them, in very fine clothes, for a social occasion, I believe.

Upon his return with Mr. Charles and the sisters, I sensed a great deal of agitation in him. Though he went to bed after some snappy, incomprehensible conversation with the rest of the company, he never slept a wink the whole night. He was up again before sunrise, and off he went, this time on horseback, without me.

Why do humans do things that make them so unsettled? I don't have that problem. In fact, I will stop worrying about it and take a nice, long nap.

Fitzwilliam Darcy

Netherfield, October 14

How do I put down on paper the jumble of emotions that have tossed me like a ship in a storm in the last twelve hours? I must organize my thoughts and take a rational approach. None of this should be causing me the least bit of unrest, and yet I am perturbed. I must analyze all this rationally.

First, I am afraid I must have looked somewhat foolish at that confounded Assembly last night. I hate nothing more than opening myself up to the commentaries of fools, but what else might I expect from a country assembly?

Bingley has just hinted this afternoon, during a postmortem of the evening, and the sisters have confirmed, that I was the object of much speculation and expectations last night. As I had dreaded. Apparently, I did not please the rabble because I did not dance enough, talk enough, or smile enough. I was deemed to think myself above my company.

What happened was that a rumor ran about the room as soon as we had entered—probably sparked by that Lucas fellow, who simply talks too much— that I was a most wealthy man who was searching across the kingdom for a seductive Cinderella to be my true love; and it was quite disappointing to the hopefuls that I did not immediately fix my head and heart (not to mention fortune) on an object.

The truth is that the place was noisy and crowded, the candles smoked, the musicians were more eager than able, and as soon as I walked in, I heard an old woman whisper theatrically *"TEN THOUSAND A YEAR"* into the ear of another hag while staring at me.

I wanted to turn on my heels and spend a quiet evening at home reading, sleeping, playing solitaire, anything, really. Even a reading of a few of John Donne's sermons would have been the summit of felicity compared to this.

Although I had hoped that here in the country, as a relative unknown, I might be safe from the London set, I realized I was wrong. Here again, nubile girls would be thrown in my way, their mothers eagerly projecting what luxurious toilettes and carriages would be theirs as the companions of my wealthy life. Another Amanda Edwards would be conjured up, with her coquettish ways. More false declarations, artificial emotions, stupid babble, and fakeries. I honestly think I did try to see what Miss Edwards had to offer; but there was no substance there, nothing to talk about; the same platitudes and idiocies that plague bored, so-called "accomplished" women. I am determined to spare Georgiana that fate.

Four times in the last five years, I have been accused (though not always openly) of toying with a woman's affections only to reject her coldly. Yet, each time, I had given very little encouragement, for a very good reason. I felt perhaps some attraction, but never attachment. I am a man, and subject to the foibles of my sex. But it is my duty to be extremely careful in my assessment of a woman's suitability. For this reason, I do not banter, I do not flirt, I do not pay false compliments, I do not blather and bumble and make an idiot of myself simply to please a woman.

I know it is my duty to provide heirs for Pemberley. I am also aware of certain familial schemes that would aggrandize our holdings with a sizable property in Kent. But I have no wish to become a traveling landowner, and Pemberley is quite enough for my stewardship. And I have no intention of marrying my poor cousin Anne only to palliate my aunt's ardent anxieties. I refuse to—but I am veering off topic. I must go back to the matter at hand.

So, to return to the Assembly. I stood aghast after hearing that whisper, which cut me like the lash of a vicious whip. I walked about, quite angry that I could never be anything but the Man with Ten Thousand a Year. I looked around me and saw vulgar faces, conceited airs, pretentious nobodies, buffoons, wags, hags, and fools.

But those were only my first impressions. For soon afterwards, something caught my eye. Something—or rather Some One. My eyes were struck by a lovely creature. It was visible from her fresh countenance and sweet deportment that none of the peevish manners and egotistical sentiments that form the backbone of Miss Edwards (and her sister) could ever reside within this person. But no sooner had I laid eyes on her and recovered from my surprise at finding so much beauty in this setting than I perceived that Bingley had seen and felt the same as I—and the lady was returning his unabashedly admiring stares with very pretty smiles indeed. Not that she acted the coquette. She had an air of genuineness that was exceedingly appealing. I was moved by her appearance and felt the sting of seeing that she found Bingley more to her liking than she did me. Indeed, the feeling in my breast was so violent that it rather shocked me, although I took care not to reveal the turmoil that rocked me, and I was able to maintain a serene countenance. After a while, I was even able to take considerable pleasure in watching her dance. She had a queenly deportment but the candid air of a shepherdess from a poem of yore.

Bingley asked her to dance twice, and if propriety had allowed it, I do believe he would have danced with no one else all evening. But Bingley is a brave lad who knows his duty, and he paid attention to as many of his new neighbors of the female sex as possible by dancing. To those of the male sex, he paid the compliment of conversing. Of what insipid elements these conversations consisted, I dare not speculate. He did interrupt his social frolicking long enough to come chide me for my lack of participation in the revelries. Had HE walked the breadth and length of the many lanes in the Netherfield woods that afternoon, as I had, perhaps he might have better understood my reluctance to dance. But as this is quite a paltry excuse, I did not voice it.

In fact, I am deceiving myself. I was not all that fatigued. Had that lovely girl looked at me the way she did at Bingley, I believe I could have conjured up the energy to stand up with her…all night.

"Come, Darcy, you must dance!" said Bingley to me during a pause in his exertions. I had already performed my duty by his sisters and was in no mood to tire myself further with a woman who would turn out to be another Miss Edwards. In what I hoped would be a light tone, I replied that he had appropriated the only beautiful woman in the room, to which he readily acquiesced, bursting into a panegyric of the young lady's perfections.

"Well, why would you punish me by having me dance with others when you have reserved the best for yourself?" I retorted.

"Darcy, there are a dozen charming girls here. Some seem to be lacking partners," he said, glancing sidelong at a group of women who were sitting out the dance. As he continued babbling, I followed his gaze, hardly paying attention to his words. The three girls he was so helpfully pointing out were nothing to the lovely creature he had claimed. Two of the young ladies were decidedly plain. The third, a little less so, but still—

"Yes, tolerable, I suppose, but not handsome enough to tempt me," I said, wishing to be playful, but my speech came out sounding serious and harsh. Bingley shook his head and rejoined the frolickers. *Not handsome enough to tempt me as your lovely partner is tempting me*, I should have said. But it would not do to cast myself as Bingley's rival. And so, I remained a silent spectator for the rest of the evening.

Her name is Miss Bennet. Miss Jane Bennet. She is the eldest of five sisters, and her father is a country gentleman residing several miles from Netherfield. Given Bingley's evident infatuation, I do not doubt that we shall see more of that family in the near future.

Why does it give me pain to think that Charles will be courting the beautiful Jane, that she will return his affection, and that I will be unable to do anything about it? Ah, I must put all this out of my head. I am not being rational.

Georgiana Darcy

Pemberley, October 25

We have had five days of unceasing rain, and I think I shall soon go mad if nothing happens soon. I hate these dark days of autumn. With Willy and the visitors gone, I feel like an abandoned princess in a castle that has fallen asleep. Why could I not go with them to Hertfordshire? But I know the answer to that question, of course. I have nothing but my own ignorance and stupidity and foolishness to blame. It's no use sighing over this. But I cannot help feeling a little sorry for myself—although I have no time for pulling a long face. Mrs. Annesley will be coming in a few minutes, and I must get back to my studies. The Glorious Revolution. Oh bother! Glorious indeed! Mrs. Annesley is kind, but I long for other company. I wish I could have gone to Hertfordshire. I wish I had a sister. Or two. Or ten. I wish my life were different.

Fitzwilliam Darcy

Netherfield, October 30

The two eldest Bennet sisters visited Louisa and Caroline here yesterday, and I was not surprised to see Charles still quite admiring of the lovely Jane. Always the perfect host, he insisted on showing his guests the many attractions of the house. They enjoyed his bubbling, loquacious energy, one thing I envy him for. He has a wonderful, infectious laughter. I am happy to have him for a friend, despite his obnoxious sisters.

Jane Bennet looked enchanting. She wore a simple muslin frock and a bonnet that Louisa later declared she must have made herself, but her tall stature, regal deportment, and sweetness of manner are an irresistible combination. I tried not to stare at her too much; in fact, I only stole a few glances now and then. I watched Bingley narrowly. Utterly smitten! Ah, Bingley… Always falling in love, and out. If he does fall out…perhaps Jane is not lost to me yet. But I felt a bit oafish, standing about and saying very little, while Bingley bantered on like a lovable hero in a Goldsmith play.

Jane's sister Elizabeth is not a beauty, as there are imperfections in her that deny her the title. She is shorter than Jane. Her forehead is a bit too rounded, her nose too pert, her mouth perhaps too wide, too mobile. However, she surprised me by her desire to linger in the library, where she eyed with unconcealed delight the many volumes and said not a word to me for nearly ten minutes—she might as well have been quite alone—while the rest of the party went on to the gallery and perhaps, who knows, to some crenellated archer's walk or dark dungeon. I felt I had to keep "Lizzie," as her sister calls her, company. And so, for sport, eventually I adroitly quizzed her on a few authors. I was astonished to find her uncommonly conversant in literary matters. It seems not all girls are dunces. Perhaps in these country villages there is not much to do. And so, Miss Elizabeth Bennet reads.

I will be dissatisfied if Georgiana does not keep up with her reading. I left Mrs. Annesley with quite a list.

Georgiana Darcy

27

Pemberley, October 30

A letter came from Willy, and he has made me so happy! He is to take me to London this winter and has promised to engage a music teacher of "the highest caliber, to do justice to your talent and application" as he so kindly put it. I have been so remiss in my practice in the last few weeks, ever since he left to accompany the Bingleys to their new residence in Hertfordshire. I am ashamed of my listlessness. It is time for me to go practice. Practice, practice, practice. A good way to make the tedious hours go by a bit faster.

Fitzwilliam Darcy

Netherfield, November 4

This evening, I was persuaded by Bingley to accompany him and his sisters to Sir William Lucas's "large Party." Though social engagements are not my favorite way to pass the time, I did not need much prodding. I have to admit that I wanted to see more of Miss Bennet. Bingley talked to me as sternly as he could and made me promise to at least TRY to be civil with his neighbors. I laughingly agreed. I am not so devoid of knowledge and manners as to be the oaf that the entire county believed me to be after that silly Assembly. There is nothing wrong with a little reserve. In fact, in some individuals it is lacking to a most singular degree and should be encouraged rather than condemned.

To Lucas Lodge we therefore repaired. In the carriage, Louisa and Caroline cackled with glee, predicting all the horrors they would encounter at this fellow's fête.

"That poor old maid daughter of his! So ill-favored by nature! Squinty-eyed, and such a nose! I wonder how she will dress her hair tonight! Feathers, or a fruit cornucopia?" Louisa said, provoking screeching laughter from Caroline.

"He will surely talk of his knighting again," Caroline said. "Is there anything more insupportable than these country squires' sense of self-importance? Mr. Darcy, you are very quiet. I am sure you are dreading this little assembly as much as Louisa and I are!"

"Darcy is probably quiet because you and Louisa have been so incessantly abusing our new neighbors that nobody can place a word in," Bingley said, a little out of humor.

"Come, Charles, we know of at least ONE new neighbor—a certain Miss Bennet? —that we shall not dare abuse; at least not in your presence," Louisa said.

"Nor out of it, I hope," I interjected. I am not sure what irritated me more, their sense of superiority, their sneering tone, or the actual words that poured out of their unkind mouths. They had some measure of audacity, to insinuate that Miss Bennet should deserve abuse. Miss Bennet is far prettier, and I daresay better mannered, than these two silly geese.

I truly hoped I might engage her in conversation this evening.

"Mr. Darcy, of course not. Louisa and I agree that Miss Bennet is a sweet girl. I am not ashamed to have her as an acquaintance. But what do you gentlemen say of her younger sisters?"

Charles and I remained silent. I had to admit that what I had seen of the youngest three, though it was little, was not encouraging. Two of them at least should not be allowed out in society, given their youth and impudent manners. The third has a pinched air and speaks in supercilious, sententious tones. Eliza Bennet is more acceptable, however, and seems to at least have some sense and some education.

"The sisters, aye, but let us not forget the mother!" Louisa added. They continued with their remarks while Bingley and I remained unresponsive to their chatter.

At Sir William's, Bingley immediately attached himself to Miss Bennet. She seemed quite polite and appropriately receptive of his attentions, but my heart does not detect that she is as taken by him as he is by her. I felt a renewal of hope. I would simply have to be patient.

I was left to make my own way in the crowd. I was amused to see that Sir William displays the same ostentatious taste in his small rooms as does my Aunt Catherine in her splendid chateau. A lot of gilding and ponderous draperies and velvet. A mismatched riot of colors and patterns in the upholstery. After a while, however, I became bored with judging the furniture. Remembering my promise to Bingley, I decided that I should pay more attention to the host and guests. I approached a cluster of officers and ladies that included Miss Elizabeth Bennet. The conversation was lively, owing to her, it seemed. She has a decidedly playful demeanor. I saw her interlocutors guffaw at some witticism of hers. I decided to join them and listen.

"Miss Lizzie" turned to me abruptly soon after my approach, and looking steadfastly into my eyes boldly asked what I thought of her turn of phrase in addressing Colonel Forster. I was a bit surprised, but I responded gamely. We had barely exchanged a few sentences when Miss Lucas, whose hair looked rather nice, despite Louisa's predictions of plumage and pears, arrived and forcibly dragged her friend Eliza to the pianoforte to play.

The eldest Miss Bennet, I have been told, does not play or sing in company, which is regrettable. Among the five sisters, only Miss Elizabeth Bennet and the middle one—the truly plain one—do. I am accustomed to excellent playing and singing, so I rather dreaded this performance. Georgiana is, I am happy to say, quite accomplished in this regard, and tackles the most arduous compositions with intrepidity. Her playing is accurate and fluid, and though her voice is not yet very strong, she has feeling and grace. I am quite proud of Georgiana. I cannot seriously expect all young ladies to be as talented and zealous as she is, so I usually brace myself for inferior playing in society, especially in the country, and I try to summon up charitable thoughts on those occasions. I walked quietly away toward the punch bowl.

I had another surprise in store. Miss Elizabeth does not play as well as Georgiana, that is true, and the piece she performed is several levels of difficulty below what my sister tackles with ease, but there was something about her expression, the purity of her voice, that moved me as she sang. I forgot about the punch, turned around, and walked back slowly to watch and listen.

Unfortunately, my pleasure was rather short-lived, because as soon as she had done, the plain sister rushed to take her place and started plucking away at the keys and butchering what might have been a love song; her voice inflated and screeched in the high tones, groaned in the middle, disappeared in the low, and hiccoughed in between.

I quickly walked away again, embarrassed for her, and most perplexed. How could one sister create such delight and another such agony? To lack talent and not recognize it must be one of the most sinister tricks Nature can play on us. But she was soon interrupted: the two youngest sisters demanded a reel and set up dancing, to everyone's relief, though I cannot think what polite society would think of this sort of wild revelry, and I was disappointed not to hear more of Miss Lizzie's voice. I was contemplating some scheme to bring her back to the instrument, when Sir Lucas approached me and badgered me with rather impertinent questions, which I answered as succinctly as possible. At one point, Miss Elizabeth was making her way, I think toward Miss Lucas, when he intercepted her thus:

"Miss Eliza, why aren't you dancing? Mr. Darcy, may I commend this very desirable partner to you." He took her hand and nearly placed it into mine, which unconsciously I had proffered to the lady.

At this moment, dancing with Miss Eliza Bennet seemed a better occupation than continuing a conversation with this pompous fool, and I smiled at her, almost in gratitude. But she swiftly removed her hand and stated with great energy, if some confusion, that she did not have the least intention of dancing.

"But my dear Eliza, though he dislikes dancing, Mr. Darcy is very willing."

"Mr. Darcy is all politeness," she replied, looking at me steadily. Her gaze locked with mine. I was struck by the beauty of her dark eyes, the fineness of her eyelashes. As if I had never seen them properly before. But the moment passed. She smiled and turned away. A few seconds later, she and Miss Lucas were conversing, and I watched them calmly, remaining silent until Sir William, out of topics, decided to go harass another guest.

But it seems I was not to be left alone this evening. Caroline came next, gliding toward me with her long neck outstretched like a goose flying south. "My poor Mr. Darcy. Can you believe our situation? I am appalled. You look pensive. I think I know why," she declared.

"I should imagine not."

"You are thinking how low-bred this company is and how insupportable it would be to pass many more evenings in this fashion."

"No. My mind was more agreeably engaged," I replied. And then I told her that I was reflecting on the pleasure that a man can derive from contemplating a pair of fine eyes in a woman's pretty face. And when she inquired as to whose eyes, I did not lie. I identified the owner of the fine eyes. Which left her quite astonished but not too stunned to omit making a sarcastic remark. I am not sure why I exposed this feeling to Caroline, who I am sure will make much of it. Perhaps I did it to annoy her. And of course, I am safe in the knowledge that I have seen many pairs of beautiful eyes and that those of Miss Elizabeth Bennet pose no threat to me.

Georgiana

Pemberley, November 6

Something unexpected and frightening happened today. The rain let up a bit this morning, and I was allowed to go walking on my own for once, since Mrs. Annesley was feeling poorly. As I was going down the path leading to the orchard, one of the undergardeners—I think his name is Barrows—came toward me. He raised his cap. He had an alarmed and furtive look. Of a sudden he said, "Please take this Miss," and he handed me a letter! After which he ran off. I was so surprised. I almost felt faint when I saw the hand. It was from George. I knew I should not open it. I knew I should deliver it immediately to Mrs. Annesley to remit to my brother upon his return. But I am still, it seems, very wicked. I opened it, and I read it.

My dear, lovely Georgiana,

> *My heart aches from your silence. You know I cannot live without your regard. I have been wandering as in a desert for many months since Fate (and Fitzwilliam) cruelly banished me. You and I have been friends for so long. At Ramsgate, I thought you had understood what I desired from you; but I fear you dreadfully misinterpreted my message. To my horror, you ran to the protection of Fitzwilliam as if I intended to do you harm!*
>
> *My dear, dearest Georgiana, there are some things that we learn as we get older that are so difficult to explain in a mere letter, and that is what I hoped to do, tell you the truth, explain to you in person, at Ramsgate, certain events that have come to light—but your Brother came upon us before I could—Oh, I cannot continue. The burden of my soul is unbearable. The considerable boxing I received from Fitzwilliam is nothing compared to the knowledge that you think me a blackguard. Though I am sure my jaw still aches from the punishing blows. I believe it was fractured. I did not dare fight back. I could not hurt him—could not hurt my childhood friend, the son of my benefactor, and your beloved Brother.*

Please give me another chance to explain. I know there is still time for you to understand.

As I received intelligence that your Brother would be away for a few weeks, I took the liberty—forgive my forwardness—to try to communicate with you. I am taking the risk of being discovered and chased off Pemberley to have this message delivered to you, though I know not when it may finally reach you. Yet I will wait, and I will hope.

Georgiana, you must allow me the opportunity to set things straight. You cannot be so cruel as to abandon me to a life of calumny and slurs. As it is, I believe my days may be numbered. I live, I breathe, only so that I can speak the truth to you. Otherwise, death is imminent. Who will grieve for me when I am gone?

If you have any fondness left in your heart for your dear childhood friend, please meet me by the stream—where we built the little wooden bridge, years ago… Be assured you will be safe, you could not be safer with anyone else. If you will do me this justice—for you are a young woman of character and righteousness—please leave a ribbon at your window at night—any night. The next day, I will be there from sunup to sundown, waiting for you.

How my heart beat as I read this letter! But I could not untangle my feelings. I do not know if I love, hate, despise, pity, or admire George. And is it possible that my brother would have done violence to him, as he claims? What does he mean, that his days may be numbered? Is he in earnest?

I am in such turmoil. If only my brother were here—but would I dare to ask him what really happened at Ramsgate? What slurs does George speak of? My brother assured me that I had done the right thing by going to him, but sometimes I think I was a fool for turning to Willy so quickly. I should have taken matters in hand myself. I was scared. I wish I were braver. I wish I knew my own mind better. Oh, if only I had someone I could talk to!

I know what I ought to do now—tell all to Willy—but I am tempted to go to the bridge tomorrow. If only to hear what George has to say. I do owe him that. And with death imminent? Yes, there could be no wrong in that! Except if Willy finds out—but why should he?

I must be brave! I shall meet George at the little bridge tomorrow at sunup. I *shall* be brave!

The setting sun is casting a brilliant light as I am finally alone in my room. And to the cross pane in the window I have attached the gold and lilac ribbon I wore on my bonnet in Ramsgate when last I saw George. It flutters in the breeze, as does my heart.

Fitzwilliam Darcy

Netherfield, November 11

Today, as we had returned from our morning walk, when Bingley remarked to me for the hundredth time what I have been thinking myself, about how angelic Miss Bennet is, I casually told him that if he is indeed so besotted with her, he should try to relieve himself of his suffering by getting to know the lady better. I am afraid I sounded a bit cynical. I could have told myself the same thing.

"Nothing will dull her sparkle more effectively than spending more time conversing with her," I said. "You will discover that she has little to talk about that makes sense, and after a while you will find even her gracious smiles insipid."

At that moment, I noted that Caroline and Louisa had come in. They had caught the end of my little speech.

"Are you talking about Miss Bennet again? Really, Mr. Darcy, you have no compassion!" Caroline cried.

Louisa chimed in. "Do you mean to thus catalogue all women, or just those in the country?"

"I am not cataloguing anybody, just making a statement of what I expect to happen. Your brother seems to think Miss Bennet an angel. I say she is a pretty girl, nothing more. Charles, I remind you that you were quite besotted with Miss Julia Edwards a few months ago, but that soon passed. I grant you Miss Bennet may be handsomer than Miss Julia Edwards, but will she have any more wit?"

Caroline said that perhaps it was unfair to match a country wench against a superior London woman. Bingley turned a bit red in the face but stood his ground.

"Why would a London woman be necessarily superior to a woman brought up in the country? I say they can be absolute equals in terms of mental vivacity. And you must admit Miss Bennet surpasses Miss Julia Edwards—*and* Miss *Amanda* Edwards, Darcy,"—this with a knowing and teasing look in my direction—"about ten times over in beauty and in the sobriety and charm of her manners."

"To be sure, she is quite prettier than Miss *Amanda* Edwards," Caroline said. I did not quite like her tone and her sidelong glance in my direction, and I was further alarmed when I saw a wicked grin spread across her face. "But why not put Mr. Darcy's theories to the test, Charles? I propose that Louisa and I begin the process for you, invite your Angel, and see what stuff she is made of; quiz her; find out her accomplishments. What say you, Louisa?"

"A capital idea! Oh, do not make such a face, dear brother. We will behave. We will take the best care of your new favorite. Caroline, since the gentlemen are dining out with the officers tomorrow, shall we make a ladies' day of it and invite the dear Miss Bennet?"

With smirks and stifled laughter, they set immediately to penning the invitation. I moved away, closer to the hearth. Bingley joined me, still a bit ruffled.

"You see how it is, Darcy," he said in a low voice. "I divulge the slightest inclination toward a woman, and my sisters take it upon themselves to prod and cross-examine the poor defenseless lady. Should we allow this?"

I was in fact vexed to think that Miss Bennet would be in the clutches of Bingley's sisters. But they are *his* sisters, and so I smiled at him, gave a noncommittal shrug, and held my tongue. He sighed but did nothing to stop them. I suppose perhaps I should have done something. But I must own to myself the truth: I hoped that we would come back from dining with the officers (not my favorite company) early enough that I would have a chance to see Miss Bennet. The lovely, angelic Miss Bennet, who has kept me awake more nights than I would wish.

Gulliver

Netherfield, November 12

Oh, I just love it here. Lots of birds. Also, plenty of visitors, and none of them have been as disagreeable and unreasonable as that mushroom girl. I thought it would be a boring day, because it was raining hard, and that usually means that Master Willy does not take me out for our walk. So, he just let me out in the courtyard for a bit. So refreshing! I don't know why people don't like rain and mud.

I smelled them a good ten minutes before they appeared. A new horse, with a girl on it. I recognized her; she came to visit once. When she dismounted, I saw that she was soaked through, but when I came bounding toward her, she put out both her hands and scratched me right behind the ears. Great girl. But I sensed something wrong with her, which made me sad.

November 13

The nice and pretty girl is Miss Jane B. There is talk in the kitchen that she is not well. I knew it when I first caught whiff of her. I'm rarely wrong about these things. She spent the night here. I don't know how long she is staying. They have assigned a maid to her, a shrew who won't let me into the room.

Master Willy and the rest of them seem anxious and jittery, except for the fat man who drinks and sleeps; he simply drinks and sleeps. I don't like him much. He just shooed me away from my favorite spot in front of the fire. I retreated behind Master Willy's chair, and I listened. I understand the sisters and Master Willy and Mr. Charles have been arguing over the merits of Miss Jane. I did notice that Master Willy emits that new, singular, undulating yet sharp wave when Miss Jane is mentioned. And at other times too.

November 14

Yesterday a most entertaining event occurred. I was out with Master Willy. We had done the sunup-to-sundown rabbit hole quadrangle loop. I almost caught a sparrow. We were returning to the courtyard. I caught the scent immediately. Something like Miss Jane, but different, more spiky, more sing-songy, less willowy.

I loped around the chestnut grove, raced ahead, and there she was. I could tell she was friendly. Like Miss Jane, she gave me a great petting-scratching with lots of cooing. Unfortunately, I forgot about the mud I had trodden and, alas, placed my front paws on her coat, right on her belly. No matter, she laughed out loud! Master Willy was running behind me and stopped so abruptly when he emerged from the shrubbery and saw us, I thought he would topple over. But he recovered himself. He walked toward us. The girl gasped when she saw him. He had that crooked smile of his as he bowed to her. She is Miss Eliza. Miss Jane's sister. Very likeable too.

The strange thing was that I caught a new wave from Master Willy. It is quite unknown, very puzzling. I need to analyze it. What could it be? What is happening to my master? Perhaps a good nap will bring answers.

Georgiana

I have been remiss in keeping a faithful account of all that has occurred. It is not for want of zealousness but for want of courage, or perhaps lack of clarity in my thoughts.

I did go to the little bridge the morning after I set the ribbon in my window. My heart was pounding with terror on two counts as I absconded from the kitchen garden: first, I was afraid that Mrs. Annesley would look in on me, although she is not an early riser, but other people's solid habits have a way of being instantly broken when you least want them to; more importantly, I both dreaded and desired this interview with George. I half hoped that he would not be there, but true to his word, there he was, waiting by the willow bridge that he and Willy built many years ago, when I was about six years old.

Those were happier days, when they were still friends. I remember the little brook singing, my delight in splashing them both as they trod barefoot in the running water to set up the structure. If only we could go back to those times. I never understood what happened to make George go away after Father died. I was at Aunt Catherine's when it happened. When I returned, Willy was distraught. We were both heartbroken, of course, but I sensed that there was something else bothering him, a preoccupation, an unwillingness to speak. He was kind to me, as always, but he said very little, and he responded evasively to my questions about where George was.

Poor Willy. He has suffered two great losses. He was just 13 when our mother died. I was still very small—I do not remember her at all. It must have been dreadful for him. And then Father taking ill suddenly five years ago, and leaving Willy to handle everything.

It must have been so difficult. I would see Willy in the gallery, staring at the portraits of our parents for hours on end. I could not be sure if he looked sad or angry. Perhaps both.

A few months after Father's funeral, he finally told me that George was pursuing law at Oxford but that he would be in no position to receive letters from me and that he would have no time to come to Pemberley, perhaps for a very long time indeed. I found it very strange. Mrs. Annesley told me not to be so inquisitive. I folded his memory in my heart. Until I saw him again last summer at Ramsgate.

And now what George has revealed to me changes everything. So shocking! So dreadful! But in my heart, I know he must have been telling the truth. So, I told him where Willy is. George will find Willy and explain. I am not sure what will ensue. I am afraid Willy will not accept it. I would like to help, but I promised George faithfully never to breathe a word of any of this to Willy, until all is set right again. But I may have done something very wicked. George's accents rang true and his dark brown eyes held mine and did not flinch. But did I do the right thing in trusting him? In revealing the whereabouts of Willy? A new fear now besets me, that Willy may never forgive me for this. I would never be able to bear that unhappiness.

Fitzwilliam Darcy

Netherfield, November 14

I was more pleased by our meeting with the officers yesterday than I had expected. Captain Pratt and I fell into easy conversation, as he too hails from Derbyshire. He is well-spoken and well-informed, and I will not be sorry to continue the acquaintance.

We will soon be summoned to dinner. I have taken extra care with my appearance this evening, though I am not sure why. Perhaps because Miss Elizabeth Bennet is here, and I have noticed that she is quite observant. Her eyes, unlike those of her sister Jane, meet mine with intrepidity, and I am not sure what her glances convey. She is presumably to stay here a few days while Miss Bennet recovers. We have not seen the ill lady at all, as Bingley and I were out when she arrived, and she took ill very quickly.

Bingley is agitated. He can't sit still, pesters the maids as they come down from Miss Bennet's room, asking if they have made quite sure her fire is faithfully fed, whether Miss Bennet has been able to take any sustenance, whether she has been able to leave her bed. His disquietude is endearing but a little dispiriting to me. It seems he is quite taken with Jane Bennet; perhaps more so than with any other lady before. I do not wish to be his rival. But I confess I am still under the spell of her smiles and soft eyes.

The lovely autumn weather has now left us, and after two days of rain, it turned quite cold overnight. 'Tis lucky for Miss Eliza that it was not quite so cold when she was scampering about the countryside, yesterday; although, had it been frostier, there might have been less mud and she might have looked a little less unkempt when she arrived, having come—on foot—to see her sister.

It must be a good three or four miles from Longbourn to Netherfield. I had noted yesterday on my short walk with Gulliver that the rain had turned the lanes quite soggy; therefore, it was a great surprise to see Miss Eliza appearing from the woods, looking like an elf, cheeks glowing, her long chestnut hair curling wildly about her temples and shoulders as Gulliver gave her an untidy welcome, which, astonishingly, she did not seem to mind. I went back into the cover of the lanes before she saw me, but then I was startled to see that she had run, yes, literally run with Gulliver around the property, and I came upon her suddenly. When she perceived me, she seemed flustered, and she hurried to pull her hair back and tie her bonnet back on. I am afraid there was not much she could do about the mud on her coat and the dirt on her stockings and skirts.

On that account, Louisa and Caroline have been merciless; but I do not mind their gossip much, as long as I do not have to participate. It keeps their tongues occupied, and I find myself less obliged to keep up any pretense at conversation with them, as their wit flows unimpeded.

November 14, Late

It is nearing midnight, but I am not ready to seek slumber.

Miss Eliza Bennet came down from nursing her sister and joined us for supper tonight. I was a bit surprised to hear her voicing opinions that are rather out of the norm. Hurst, in a rare moment of loquacity, was singing the praises of the ragout that he had been served at Rosings a year ago. The man lives to eat, drink, play cards, and sleep, so I suppose it is not surprising that he finally deigned to add his voice to the conversation since it concerned filling his belly. Miss Eliza did not agree with his statement that the human body can stay healthy only when fed with the most refined of cuisines.

"That may be for some," she stated. "But I find that plainer dishes agree with most people best, and you do not often find those afflicted with gout, who eat food as close as possible to what was available in the Garden of Eden."

"You would prefer apples and a boiled pigeon to dishes perfected by French cooks? To a ragout de porc à la sauce Robert?" he queried, astonished.

"I would indeed," she said, smiling.

Hurst made a grimace, huffed, and turned squarely away from Miss Eliza. I felt his rudeness and was a bit distressed for her. But she seemed unruffled, caught my eye, shrugged slightly, and smiled. She does have lovely eyes. Their expression is uncommonly intelligent, and her eyelashes are dark, thick, and long. They form a pleasing contrast to her pale complexion. (By the bye, perhaps it was a mistake that I shared this observation with Miss Bingley; she has been quite relentless in sprinkling the words "fine eyes" into her conversation lately, regardless of the topic.)

Later in the evening, Miss Eliza came back downstairs and declined to join us in loo, saying she would not stay long on account of her sister and that she preferred a book, to Hurst's evident surprise and renewed disgust. I had brought into the room a few of the volumes that she had taken particular notice of when Bingley gave his tour of Netherfield, and upon reading the titles, she glanced at me somewhat quizzically from across the room, as if she was surprised that I had listened to her when we were in the library and that I had remembered the tomes that interested her. I looked down, as if engrossed by my hand of cards. I wondered what she was thinking. A few minutes later, when Caroline was praising the library at Pemberley (which she has perhaps *seen* but certainly not *profited* from) and stating that I was always buying books, Miss Eliza looked up and at me with what looked like interest. She does seem to be a true bibliophile. Quite the rarity.

The conversation turned from books to a discussion of accomplished women. Miss Eliza Bennet's declaration that my definition of an accomplished woman was too strict to allow even one woman to fit the bill was met with outright derision and scorn by Caroline and Louisa. But she held firm and simply smiled; and I was secretly amused to think that the deriders had probably read much less in their lifetimes than this saucy Miss Eliza reads in any given month. Well, after a short while, Miss Eliza left to retire for the night, and I was able to concentrate more fully on the game of loo, without fearing to look up from the card table to see her dark eyes upon me.

Gulliver looks at me quizzically. He is not accustomed to seeing me write late into the night. But again, this evening, sleep eludes me.

November 15, Nearing Midnight

I have a bit to catch up on. We were visited by a few more Bennets yesterday. It was shortly after breakfast, and I was not able to escape the intrusion of Mrs. Bennet and the two youngest sisters, who arrived to look in on the invalid.

It was an irritating visit. Mrs. Bennet borders on, or should I say, seems to cultivate vulgarity and has taken a personal dislike to me that she takes no pains to conceal. She found it incumbent upon herself to upbraid me at every turn of the conversation. I decided I would speak no more and turned away. If these are the country manners that Bingley finds so endearing, I will gladly pass such charms up. I could tell, however, that Miss Elizabeth Bennet was mortified by her mother's behavior. She occasionally glanced at me, biting her lips, as if to entreat me to pay no attention to this maternal folly. At one point, Mrs. Bennet was blathering on about the superior beauty of her eldest (which I do not dispute) in terms that were excruciatingly self-serving, no doubt directed at Charles.

"A gentleman in town was so very much in love with her," she boasted, "that we were certain he was going to make her an offer, but finding her too young perhaps, contented himself with writing a beautiful love sonnet—"

Here Miss Eliza interrupted, and I could not help admiring her adroitness in turning the conversation from the specific (and insolent) to the general (and philosophical).

"And there ended his affection. I wonder who first discovered how useful poetry can be in chasing love away," she declared.

I joined back into the conversation, to tease her a bit, saying I had always considered poetry the food of love, to which she made a witty reply. Miss Eliza understands how variable this thing called "love" can be among humans—how flimsy sometimes.

She spoke the truth. There is a fine line between affection and affectation, and I find I am not adept at properly deciphering what ladies project and what they really feel. I pondered her reply, while the youngest—I believe she is the youngest, though she is very tall and by far the most forward, nay, most impudent young lady I have ever met with—a great contrast to Georgiana, though they are probably about the same age—well, this Lydia started badgering Charles about giving a ball at Netherfield. To my dismay, he responded with enthusiasm, and so I fear I will not be able to escape another evening of society in this rusticity. The two girls and their mother departed noisily, Caroline and Louisa hardly able to conceal their contempt as Mrs. Bennet obsequiously thanked and re-thanked her dear Mr. Bingley.

How Miss Bennet and Miss Eliza have turned out so well-bred is perplexing.

This evening, when Miss Eliza came down from her sister's chamber, I became aware that her presence at Netherfield is not without its advantages. Our soirées, which of late had been rather tedious, are livelier with this new addition, and it gives me some relief from Caroline's too zealous attentions toward me. It is unfortunate that the environs have not yet produced a gentleman to court her.

When Eliza Bennet joined us in the drawing room, I was writing to Georgiana. Caroline hardly acknowledged Eliza's presence. She continued pestering me with her usual vapid commentary, but at last left her post to take a look at what Miss Eliza was stitching.

"Blackwork, Miss Eliza, what a charming design. I quite dote on blackwork. Miss Darcy finished a bell pull in blackwork that is most exquisite, did she not, Mr. Darcy? Quite larger and more complex than what you are working on, Miss Eliza. Is the design yours?"

The lady replied it was not, but copied from a fashion plate.

"Indeed, Miss Eliza! I am surprised. I always use my own designs. So does Louisa. We would not be content to merely copy. But perhaps that counts not as an accomplishment in *your eyes*."

I looked over and perceived a small smile in Elizabeth Bennet's countenance. She was stolidly ignoring Caroline's poisoned darts.

"Mr. Darcy," Caroline continued, "your dear sister invents all her own embroidery designs, does she not?"

"I cannot vouch for it. I take no great interest in such matters. I am much more concerned in her being as well-read as possible. Needlework is not a priority in my view."

"Oh, but in *all* respects, Georgiana is *so* accomplished. Pray tell her I am quite enraptured with her new design for a table."

I had no room for conveying these sentiments and told her so. Annoyed with her persistence in addressing me, I put away my pen, convinced that she would not leave me uninterrupted for long. Indeed, she continued with a panegyric on my letters, then berated Charles for not being able to write half so well.

Charles often takes the bait at her criticisms, but this time he deflected the blow toward me by inferring that my style of writing was too complex, that I sought large words. I saw Miss Elizabeth smile at that. She soon joined the conversation and elevated it to such a degree that Caroline looked confused and bemused, which I found capital. Eliza threw the Bingley sisters into a deal of wretched uncertainty when she made a remark on the ambiguous virtues of *sesquipedalia verba*—referring to a conversation that she and I had had in the library, about Horace mocking pretentious writing. She looked at me archly. I had to smile at her. I was delighted to see that this Latin locution frightened Caroline, who was suddenly silent and vexed.

I was lured into pursuing the conversation. Bingley, always pleasant in his discourse, was in full form, and Miss Eliza has an address that is both playful and rhetorically flawless, something I have never before witnessed in a woman. How strange that all of London never produced (at least in my presence) what I am finding here, in the backwoods of Hertfordshire. I was a little taken aback, however, when Charles declared to all that he would readily yield to me in any dispute only because I was such a tall, frightening fellow, especially at Pemberley, "of a Sunday night, when I have nothing to do." Miss Eliza responded with an ironic smile and a raised brow toward me that seemed to say she was not one jot afraid of me.

He said this jocularly, but truth is often spoken in jest, and I was not aware that I projected this image toward *him*. 'Tis true that often, of late, I have felt restless and perhaps short tempered. If I do not fatigue myself physically during the day, I find long evenings interminable, and nights do not bring relief. That is why I did not hesitate to accompany Bingley south, despite the presence of his sisters. I am not sure if it is boredom or loneliness. Perhaps some of the melancholy humor that seemed to plague my mother has been transmitted to me. In any case, it is difficult to bear, and sometimes I feel as though I were being pushed deeper and deeper into a cave of despair.

When I first saw Miss Jane Bennet at the country assembly, it was as if a bright light had started to shine at last inside this dark cavern, indicating a way out, to verdant fields. But Miss Bennet does not seem to have felt the same thing toward me. And in my inner soul I mourn the dimming of this light.

In any case, I must brush off all this foolishness. It is of little consequence that Miss Bennet like me or not. To get back to our evening, with Caroline somewhat neutralized by her inability to follow the conversation and Bingley declaring himself unable to match Miss Eliza and me in our verbal sparring, the debate was declared a draw, I was finally able to continue my letter, and Miss Eliza returned to her blackwork.

When I had done sealing the leaves, I voiced the desire to be entertained with music. My hope was to hear Miss Elizabeth sing again, for I wanted to ascertain whether the great pleasure I had received the first time I heard her had been a momentary folly on the part of my senses. But Caroline rather impolitely hurried to the instrument, and she and Louisa triumphantly sang and played one song after another.

Miss Eliza seems to be as bored with needlework as I might be. I watched her ply the needle with no great conviction or alacrity. After a while, she put away the work and walked to the pianoforte.

I was wrong to think her figure flawed. She may not be tall, but her form is light, and she moves with grace. She does not exhibit the regal deportment of her sister Jane, but rather the sprightliness of a dancer. I was often reminded tonight, by certain expressions of hers, of the time I saw her emerging from the woods, running, with her hair loose, her cheeks brightened by her saunter. How her dark eyes sparkled that afternoon, as they did tonight by the light of the candles.

I am not quite sure what devil pushed me to join her by the piano and ask her if she would not like to dance a reel. She refused me. Playfully, but she refused me. Twice now has she turned down the opportunity to dance with me—but she was entertaining and charming enough in her response that it did not needle me as it might have.

I must confess here that I do not quite know what to make of her glances. I do not quite know what to make of Miss Eliza Bennet.

Tomorrow it is imperative that I take a very long walk with Gulliver, so I pray the weather will smile on us.

Georgiana

Pemberley, November 15

The undergardener brought me a note from George this morning. He writes with great joy, for he has found a solution! He says he will join the regiment which is quartered very near Netherfield, in a town called Meryton, and he will contrive to meet Willy. He says all will turn out well as soon as he gets a chance to talk with him. But this is all frightening to me. I am scarcely able to breathe, let alone concentrate on my Latin. Mrs. Annesley was rather bewildered by my inability to construe Pliny the Younger today, when a few weeks ago it was child's play for me.

Please, good Lord, let Willy do the right thing by George. And let George be truthful, and brave, and let Willy listen patiently, and let them not come to blows.

Fitzwilliam Darcy

Netherfield, November 16

There are strange coincidences in our lives. After my walk with Gulliver this afternoon, I received a letter from Aunt Catherine relating that her new protégé is to come to Hertfordshire to visit his cousins in a week or so. And these cousins of his happen to be no others than the Miss Bennets of Longbourn. My aunt writes thus:

"This young man has just received orders. I have generously bestowed upon him the living of Hunsford, but he is due to inherit an estate in Hertfordshire when its master, his uncle (a certain Mr. Bennet), passes on, as he has no male heirs. I find this antiquated custom of entailment detestable and altogether shockingly dishonorable to women. Therefore, I pointed out to Mr. Collins the great advantages he would find in marrying one of the Bennet sisters. I hear there are quite a few girls of marriageable age in that family, and surely among them he will find a suitable wife. I directed him to go visit them as soon as possible, make an offer, and come back engaged.

"I must speak frankly: I am not entirely satisfied with him. Although he is tall and studious, he is not handsome or clever, has little taste and less conversation, and he is not at all capable of managing the parsonage by himself. I must constantly go there in person and direct him in the minutest details. I declare, if it hadn't been for me, there would still be no shelves in the closets! But he is pious and obedient, and these are the qualities par excellence *that I demand of a curate.*

"My dear nephew, I do not expect that you should exert yourself excessively in this matter, but since I have learned that you are staying in the vicinity of this Mr. Bennet's estate—Longbourn is the name—I pray you may make discreet inquiries as to the character of the ladies in question so that Mr. Collins does not bring back a harridan or a harlot. In these times of insolence, it is becoming increasingly difficult to find women of virtue. But we must. Men, when they stay single too long, soon fall prey to innumerable vices. Your cousin

Anne, of course, is unique in possessing at once unparalleled charm and understanding..."

She continued with a catalogue of Anne's virtues. It was a poorly veiled reiteration of her wish for me to expedite a proposal to Anne. I laughed out loud when I read that letter. There is no need for me to make discreet inquiries, as I have seen enough to know that at least four of the five Bennet sisters will not be suitable for a man who is neither handsome nor clever—or rather, *he* will be unsuitable for *them.* But perhaps that plain, pretentious middle sister might be willing to take on a man so lacking in attractions. That, of course, will not do in my response to my aunt, so I shall keep it short and evasive, as usual.

However, the thought that the eldest Miss Bennet might be sacrificed to a dull clergyman for the benefit of retaining the estate for her sisters' sake did give me pause. But why should I care, really? This might be a good solution for the Miss Bennets' future. As I told Bingley and his sisters, given the inferiority of our new acquaintances' situation, there is scarcely a self-respecting gentleman who would commit the folly of marrying one of the Bennet sisters, despite sweet smiles. Or fine eyes.

November 16, Late Morning

This morning, when I looked out the window, I saw a golden mist lingering among the weeping willows by the brook. Too enticing to stay indoors! What a misfortune that Caroline intercepted me as I was trying to leave unnoticed with Gulliver! In future, I must make certain I rise earlier, to escape her company.

My regret at revealing, quite stupidly, my admiration for Miss Eliza's eyes was not ill-founded. Caroline taunted me all through our painfully slow walk in the lanes. To her jeering descriptions of my future felicity I responded only with monosyllables, shrugs, or silence. Given the frequency and tenacity of her taunts, I believe I can establish without a doubt—alas—that this lady is jealous of Miss Eliza Bennet (of all people!) on my account. Which brings me this useful lesson, that any sign of admiration toward any member of the opposite sex must be repressed and that I must be more guarded at all times in this respect. Again, as with Miss Edwards, it is a thorny road that a man of means must navigate, even in the most mundane situations.

As Caroline chattered on, leaning too heavily on my arm for my comfort, I amused myself by imagining other uxorial prospects than the one she was proposing.

Jane Bennet, as for beauty and grace—what a delightful wife she would make—but that mother of hers! Alas, Caroline is right about that!

My cousin Anne—no, a thousand times no. I do feel quite sorry for her. Poor little mouse raised by a big, loud, ferocious cat. She shrinks from all contact and is happiest when left by herself, drawing and painting. I have never exchanged more than a few desultory sentences with her.

Miss Amanda Edwards, now that I know her character, not for a kingdom! By Jove, I feel my manhood shriveling when I contemplate my misery in her company.

As for Caroline Bingley, much as I respect Charles, I'd rather not marry at all than be coupled with such a shrew and endure her pointy nose, pointy elbows, and pointy critiques forever.

November 16, Late Evening

I am aching for my bed, but I must make sense of what happened this evening.

Miss Bennet is making a good recovery. She came downstairs after dinner for the first time since she has been here. I was a bit peeved because Charles seemed intent upon keeping her to himself, and I did not wish to intrude. I observed his solicitude in keeping her warm and comfortable. His admiration for her continues and possibly has increased. She smiled wanly, and I was a little surprised to see that her looks were not as striking as I had perceived them to be at first. Perhaps it is the effect of her illness. But one thing is for certain, I did not notice any sign of great agitation in her heart toward Bingley, no great fire being stoked in her soul. She is at all times, it seems, very staid and serene. There is little excitement in her countenance; a sweet, soft look, beautiful, certainly, but... well, to my surprise and relief, I now find that my admiration for her, though still present, is completely manageable.

So. The turmoil that I was in after seeing Miss Bennet that first night is extinguished. I rejoiced in this as I sat in the drawing room, but I had to own that it was a bittersweet feeling. As if I had just sustained a loss. At any rate, thought I, it is for the best.

She is a kind, lovely, perfectly polite young lady; but I started musing that *she* would never be running through the woods after a soaking rain, without her bonnet, long locks tumbling on her shoulders, like her sister Eliza. This evening, however, I felt that Miss Eliza was looking anything but wild, plying her needle quietly as she sat across the room from me. Then, something happened. Perhaps she sensed my gaze upon her. She looked up at me briefly with those dark, mischievous eyes, and I felt—well, I felt what a man might feel when a gypsy temptress gives him a come-hither look. Throughout my body. Good Lord! I had hardly recovered from the jolt than I realized that by a great misfortune, Caroline had caught something of my turmoil. And though I plunged back into my book, I felt Caroline's sidelong stare upon me as she paraded to and fro in the drawing room.

A few minutes later, at the request of Caroline, who had been yawning loudly all evening, Miss Eliza did abandon her work, and they walked about the room together. Eventually we engaged in a new exchange, this time regarding issues of character—vanity and pride—where again Miss Eliza's rhetorical skills quite overshadowed those of Caroline, who threw sharp, narrow glances at us—which I secretly rejoiced in. And here I forgot my morning's resolution to keep aloof and quiet. Miss Eliza's playful jabs at my supposed perfection—"a man with no faults," as touted by Caroline— provoked me enough that I am afraid I made statements that now I fear were too private, too self-referential, perhaps boastful. At one point, our talk became somewhat heated, and Miss Eliza even rebuked me for "hating everyone." I do not think anyone has ever spoken so directly and forwardly to me since I was fourteen! I did not mind this direct attack, however, for I was able to give her tit for tat.

The shock of my physical reaction to the sight of her bewitching eyes had subsided a bit, and I was recovering my full powers of expression.

To tell the truth, although I resented my own weakness of flesh (as it were), I rather enjoyed having a lady not mincing words or spewing mealy whiny platitudes. My physical reaction was completely understandable, in retrospect; I liked how her eyes shone in the candlelight, like dark pools in moonlight. Her complexion is fine, her eyebrows mobile and expressive, animated with a playful insolence, and I couldn't help smiling when I told her that *her* fault lay in willfully misunderstanding everyone. I am not sure how we would have resolved this impasse if Caroline hadn't hurried to the instrument and started making great noise with it.

Georgiana

Pemberley, November 16

I have received a letter from Willy. He does not mention having seen George. I am so disappointed! I was hoping to have good news by now in that respect— I want it all settled! But I will have to be patient. I am happy at least to see that Willy is NOT interested at all in Miss Caroline Bingley. He writes:

"...I was thinking of quitting Netherfield earlier than planned, because I found myself getting somewhat restless. Netherfield is a charming estate, but the society here in the country is a little limited, as is to be expected, and thus, one evening is much like the next. I love Charles and his lively manner, but as you know, Mr. and Mrs. Hurst and Caroline Bingley can be somewhat—well, let us just say I tire of their company too quickly.

"This brings me to reiterate how much importance I place on your course of reading. I do not insist on this to be dictatorial or harsh, but because I find deplorable the results of faulty education, even in a respectable family like the Bingleys. Caroline and Louisa have very little to talk about because they have very little information, and this is because they never read. I am not accusing or judging them; indeed, they represent the norm, and they can relate anecdotes and speak of things and people sensibly, and even amusingly. But my dear Georgiana, there is so little in terms of ideas in their conversation! My strongest wish is for you to not be ordinary but instead cultivate the intellect that you have been blessed with. To be able to express oneself with exactitude and honesty is laudable; to add to it verve and wit is better; and to do it with the solid basis of information and understanding is ideal.

"As an illustration, may I describe a couple of young ladies in these parts. They are sisters, new friends of Caroline, and are staying at Netherfield for a few days. They live a few miles from here; their father is a gentleman. They are handsome, but more importantly, it is evident that they have cultivated their minds. The younger of the two is especially notable in having a rare appreciation for reading; do you know she has read all of Shakespeare, is well

acquainted with the works of Racine, Corneille, Montesquieu, and Voltaire (which she reads in French), and has a passing knowledge of Latin? She also has a fine singing voice. So, as you see, even here in the country there are a few young ladies who, like you, are serious in their studies and do not fill their heads with fluff and nonsense. I know how much you love music and I hope you keep up your practice as diligently as ever; as I said before, once we are in London this winter, you will have the best tutors available.

"Has the weather enabled you to go riding much? You know how important it is to take exercise daily. Even if it rains, so long as it is not a pouring rain, or too cold, I hope you do go out every day…" etc., etc.

So, it is clear that my brother is not at all interested in Miss Bingley. That is a relief indeed! I was a little worried when they were all here at Pemberley in July and I saw her flitting about him like a gnat! I wanted to slap her. My poor brother tries to be so circumspect—"tire of their company too quickly" indeed! What he really means is that they exasperate him with their drivel. And that Mr. Hurst is a fat, drunken oaf.

But it seems Willy has met company that he enjoys a bit more. This is the first time he has acknowledged any sort of admiration for any woman in his entourage.

I am still on pins and needles though. When will George and he meet? And then…what will happen? What if my brother rejects George, calls him a liar? My God, what then? What have I done?

Gulliver

November 16

Don't understand Master Willy, don't understand him at all. Sitting all day like a mute after what happened this morning. I sense turmoil, agitation, excitement, and I can't decide: is this good or bad? Sometimes it's like when bells ring out. Sometimes a dark rumbling like when a storm strikes. Must think about this. Here's what happened.

I was let outside, ah, the air so fresh today, and great breezes sending dead leaves in whirling fits while those hideous blackbirds cawed at me. Good! You plumed fellows want action? There I went… I chased a crow, which I would have caught, really I would, except that I was interrupted by the girl, Miss Eliza, who had come outside. She likes me! I brought a stick and dropped it at her feet. We played fetch for a good while, I took a few moments now and then to chase crows, but with no success. Anyway, Miss Eliza runs fast! and throws far! I like how she laughs, pretends to throw, hides the stick, throws it again. I'm catching on! Great time, great time.

Then, because of the direction of the wind, I did not sense that Master Willy had come out, and suddenly I heard him calling me. Miss Eliza turned bright red when she heard him, and she and I walked to the terrace, and then I saw that he looked a little strange. She and Master Willy exchanged some words. I caught that new effluvium from Master Willy.

I'm wondering…maybe he likes her too, maybe that is what that means.

So why has he been so silent all day, all afternoon, all evening? I look up at him, whine softly, and he ignores me. Nose stuck in a book and then another, even when in company. Well, there is nothing that a nap won't fix.

November 17

I was a little sad this morning because the pretty girls left. After that, Master Willy went up to his room and walked back and forth, pacing, pacing, pacing. This may be serious. I've had to follow him closely all day to make sure he is all right. Finally, this afternoon, I whined enough that he put on his boots and greatcoat, and I took him outside. I ran. He ran. We were out almost all the afternoon. Wonderful day. I hope that girl comes back.

Fitzwilliam Darcy

November 19

I thought I was miserable enough the last few days, but today reached a new height. Rarely have I felt so angry.

I must compose myself. I have already broken a nib and splattered ink over my sleeve.

Bingley and I were on our way to Longbourn this morning to inquire as to Miss Bennet's welfare, when we intercepted them in Meryton, where they were chatting with officers. To my great astonishment, among them was that villainous blackguard whose name I can hardly bear to put down on paper. He was engaged in lively conversation with Miss Elizabeth Bennet. They were a little apart from the others. I saw them from a distance. Her cheeks were quite pink. She looked pleased with him; naturally, he has winning looks and an amiable delivery, and I cannot fault her for being civil.

Bingley, of course, had trotted ahead of me as soon as he had perceived Miss Bennet. I could not turn back at that point. I slowed Cicero down to a senatorial pace. My breathing was labored. I recovered myself enough, however, to nod and address the assembled ladies and gentlemen—except, of course, I refused to acknowledge Wickham's presence.

Wickham started when he saw me. He glared intently as if to provoke me; there was an insolent bravado all over his features. I believe, had the ladies not been there, I would have struck his face over and over with my riding crop. After what he did—tried to do—to Georgiana! And now here he was currying favor with the Miss Bennets! What the deuce brings him down here? Did he know I was in Hertfordshire? I took my leave as soon as I could.

As we were riding back to Netherfield, Charles expressed his displeasure.

"Darcy, what demon possessed you? I barely had time to inquire about Miss Bennet's health, and missed being introduced to some of the officers!"

"And how is Miss Bennet?" I asked coldly.

"Much better! I was delighted to see the color restored to her cheeks."

"Indeed. Glad of it," I huffed.

"Darcy, what the devil *is* the *matter* with you?"

"Charles, you saw that man who was talking to Miss Eliza Bennet?"

"Yes?"

"That was Mr. George Wickham—yes, the son of my father's steward. The one who—the one Georgiana—" I could not finish, but since I had acquainted Bingley with the particulars of this story, with a strict injunction never to breathe a word of it to his sisters, or to anyone, I did not need to go any further.

Bingley is such a dear friend to me, and since I had absolutely no family to whom I could turn last summer—the Colonel being away in the North—and because the burden was too heavy to support on my own (I am afraid that is one of my weaknesses), I owe to him the comfort of having been able to unleash my troubles to someone I could trust. He was instrumental in helping me retain my sanity.

"Good God!" Bingley exclaimed. "Was he not supposed to have gone to sea?"

"Yes. His presence here took me by surprise; and his acquaintance with the Miss Bennets bodes very ill. You plan to invite all the officers to your ball next week, I gather?"

"Indeed, I cannot avoid it, or single him out."

"You need not worry on that account. I will make certain he makes no appearance at Netherfield."

Bingley stared at me with worry and concern, but I did not care to elaborate how I would make sure the villain stayed away.

Shortly after dusk, Carruthers came to me with a knitted brow. "If you please, Sir, I have been given this letter for you."

It was in George's hand. A few inquiries revealed that Carruthers had gotten it from the housekeeper, who had gotten it from the scullery maid, who had gotten it from a stable boy, who said he got it from a man who had been roaming the park and who fit Wickham's description.

I had no desire to pollute my senses with this letter. The scoundrel! How dare he presume to *write* to *me*? I sensed that Carruthers was far too interested in this letter. I dismissed him early, and as soon as I was alone in my chamber, I threw the vile paper, unread, into the fire.

Tomorrow I will give orders to be informed directly if this individual is ever seen here again.

I keep two pistols in good working order, and I know how to use them. Tomorrow, I will engage in a little target practice nonetheless. I am superior to Wickham in firearms as well as in swordsmanship, and he knows it.

It galls me to recall Miss Lizzie's laughter as she talked with Wickham. Not that I would ever consider him a rival, but still, I am annoyed. What is he doing here?

It has dawned on me that since I am on excellent terms with Captain Pratt, he might be persuaded to become my eyes and ears as to the doings of this good-for-nothing.

Georgiana Darcy

November 25

I received another letter from George and have been tearful all day.

He wrote that when he and Willy met by chance in the village, Willy refused to acknowledge him and looked at him in great anger. He says he received no answer to the letter he then wrote to Willy. He says he went to Netherfield again to try to deliver another, and he was told by the stable boy that Mr. Darcy would surely kill him if he ever came there again; that after he received that first letter, Mr. Darcy was seen at target practice with his pistols every day and that he and Charles Bingley had engaged in fencing. So now he does not know what to do. George sounded desperate in his letter: "… If after my revelations your brother still thinks of me as a peasant and liar, there is no more hope for reconciliation, and my life is not worth living."

I am not sure how George worded his letter to Willy, but I would not be surprised if Willy thinks that George is lying, no matter how well he presented his case. That his claims are complete fabrications. In fact, I myself do not know what to believe. When George talked to me, I was convinced of his sincerity. Was I taken in? As for Willy, as sweet and indulgent as he is with me, I know he can be severe and unyielding when his pride is at stake. And I would not be surprised if he did want to kill George. And if he does kill him, it will be my fault. Oh, what should I do?

I must go to Netherfield to prevent this carnage.

Fitzwilliam Darcy

Netherfield, November 26

Well, Pratt is proving to be an invaluable ally indeed. He has just reported that our scheme has worked perfectly, and there is no chance that Wickham will darken the hallways of Netherfield tonight, as Pratt was able to persuade Colonel Forster to send him off on a fool's errand—at my request. A fool gets his just deserts in this case; after remembering Miss Eliza's hearty laughter in his company, his seductive stance toward her before he perceived me, I was not going to let him interfere in this soiree's revelries.

It is the first time in years that I look forward to a ball. The miserable weather these last four days has left all of us eager for a little action, a little society. Poor Gulliver! He feels it too. He has been moping about, attached to my heels all day, as if following me so closely will make this dark rain let up. As soon as the weather clears, I am taking him to run the length and breadth of Netherfield Park!

But back to tonight—of course, there will be some annoyances: I will have to do my duty by Bingley's sisters. But once that is done…once that is done, I intend to ask Miss Elizabeth Bennet to dance, and to dance again, and I hope to speak with her and nobody else tonight. I would like to establish some way of having regular opportunities to converse with her in the future. I believe that I could entice her into coming every so often to Netherfield to borrow books from the ample collection there, judging from her initial delight in the Library there.

Yes, I will dance with Eliza Bennet tonight. I chuckle as I write this, because she has refused me twice already, but those instances were not formal occasions, and I think she may have been teasing me. Testing me. I believe she will be quite amazed to be thus singled out. In fact, as I recall her stirring look in my direction a few weeks back, I may not be wrong in surmising that she secretly hopes this to be the case.

I care not what people think on this occasion. I look forward to seeing her dressed in her best finery.

I am not sure why I thought her figure mediocre when I first met her, for I have spent the last couple of nights imagining how she will move through the dances, how her light, supple body will transform the staid, methodical steps of these contrived dances into a thing of beauty and grace. I do admit that her wild appearance on that wet morning, muddy petticoat, blowsy hair, drenched shoes and all, did not displease me one bit, and I am not sure which incarnation I prefer. I like the spectrum of personalities that lie hidden in that woman, and it will be good sport to uncover them. Well, enough daydreaming, I must get myself ready.

Gulliver

November 27

It's inconceivable.

I was hoping we would be going out for a long ramble, because I'm quite certain he said we would, as soon as the weather got better, but I must give up all such hopes. He is leaving tomorrow for town. I am to be sent back to Pemberley. What did I do wrong?

Yesterday evening, before the big to-do, Master Willy was looking and acting—well, I was going to say giddy, except that he is never giddy, but as close to that as he might get, now and then humming under his breath. Carruthers helped him dress, and very persnickety was my master about how he looked, changing cravats endlessly. Frankly, as humans go, I would say he looks as good as any. Then they banished me to the kitchen, where I mulled over the human condition before taking a nap.

In the middle of the night, he came to get me. We repaired to his chamber, and there was a storm on his brow. It wasn't anything I did, because he scratched me behind the ears for a long time, but then he drank a lot of wine, and sighed in a violent, unhappy, angry way. He would get up, march about like a madman, then sit down again. Pour some wine, guzzle it down. A few hours before, he was almost singing, and now he looked like he wanted to shoot a horse.

It must have to do with the crowds that came, the music, the noise, the movement. All those carriages that came and went. Maybe he doesn't like those things. I've never seen him like this.

I don't understand why humans have such elaborate rituals that make them so unhappy. As it is, I am not sure he slept much. I lay down beside the hearth. He stared into the fire, clenching his jaw. I fell asleep and didn't get up until the sun (finally!) was far up in the sky. He had fallen asleep in the armchair, half-clothed. I think his neck hurts now. And they have all decided to leave. Which is a great pity, because I know that today, yes, I would have caught one of those ugly, taunting, stinking, miserable crows.

I really don't understand humans. Maybe I will be glad to go back to Pemberley after all.

Fitzwilliam Darcy

London, December 1

We are now in Bingley's house in town. I have not been able to write for several days, and not only because of the business of traveling and settling in. The truth is I have been beside myself with frustration and anger.

To think I had been looking forward to the ball. To inviting Miss Elizabeth Bennet to dance. To talking with her, leading her to supper perhaps. To enjoying her witty repartee. To hearing her perform with that enthralling singing voice. But none of that happened, because despite my best endeavors, that scoundrel Wickham had poisoned the young lady's impressions of me. It didn't take him long. What, have they had such a long and intimate intercourse that he was able to spew his venom so effectively? How quick she was to accept his assertions as facts! It had scarcely been a matter of days since Wickham had enlisted in the militia, according to Pratt, when I first saw him talking to the Miss Bennets. How swiftly the snake worked!

One thing was certain: I could not remain at Netherfield any longer. I had no desire to see the Miss Bennets again. Or rather, I did. But I could not bear the barb of the opprobrium that Miss Eliza was charging me with. And I do not want a chance encounter with Wickham in Meryton. I fear I should kill him. I do not regret punching him in the jaw at Ramsgate. He deserved far worse. Frankly, I would love nothing better than to call him out and skewer him. But such shows of bravado are not of this age, and redcoats are all the rage. I had to go.

The Bingleys provided an excellent pretext for my quick departure.

On the morrow of the dance, as his sisters sat languidly in the drawing room, bemoaning their fatigue, commenting on the poor quality of the shaking jelly and exchanging vulgarities couched in charming language (of course) regarding the guests they had smiled upon the night before, Bingley reminded me that he had urgent business in town.

"Won't you accompany me, Darcy?" There was a thinly veiled urgency in his tone. I could see he was offering me a reprieve from the annoyance of having to deal with Caroline and the Hursts on my own, for the few days that he would be gone.

I jumped on the occasion.

"Indeed, I believe I have business in town as well, and it will make the journey more agreeable if we go together."

"Charles, how horrid! You would leave us poor females in this wilderness, alone, unprotected?" Caroline exclaimed.

"Yes, quite unprotected," said Louisa drily, glancing expressively in Mr. Hurst's direction. We all followed her gaze. The oaf had fallen asleep on the sofa and was snoring. He had gotten impossibly drunk during the ball. I had witnessed him passing out. It was just after the middle Bennet sister had been chased away from the pianoforte by her father after her hideous exhibition, and I had almost wished to follow Hurst's example.

In a fit of sudden energy, Caroline stood up. "Louisa, let's all go to town together!" she exclaimed. "After the savagery that we witnessed last night, I am more than ready to return to civilization. Do we have *your* permission, Mr. Darcy?"

"You do not need *my* permission to accompany your brother to town," I answered as politely as I could. I was hoping Charles would try to dissuade her, but he looked rather stricken and said nothing, contenting himself with stirring the fire.

Caroline had recovered her form, and she started prancing about the room. I knew another session of *persiflage* was in store. "I declare I am a little surprised at your wanting to leave the area so soon, Mr. Darcy. I daresay you and Miss Eliza Bennet formed a charming couple as you stood up together, and I wonder you did not invite her again after those two dances? For besides that clerical imbecile, who I am certain stepped on several ladies' gowns, and that Pratt fellow, I believe you were the only man to give her consequence. And you did not bestow the compliment on any other local beauty. Tell me, did you and the fine-eyed filly quarrel?"

I was taken aback. Had she witnessed our unhappy conversation and cool parting? Did nothing escape this woman's surveillance?

"Fine-eyed filly!" Louisa squealed. "Capital!"

"Quarrel? Nonsense. We had an amicable exchange. We talked of books," I said, slightly distorting the truth. I had in fact tried to engage Eliza on that topic, but to no avail. She seemed quite angry at me for having destroyed the life of George Wickham, and her head seemed filled with nothing else. God knows what the villain told her.

"I thought Miss Eliza Bennet danced divinely," said Bingley.

"Oh, Charles, I am shocked to hear you say that!" Caroline exclaimed. "I cannot believe that you ever laid eyes on any of the dancers, save for the angelic Miss Jane Bennet. I daresay you hardly noticed her Mama getting tipsy, her young sisters chasing the officers, and the shrill squawking of yet another Bennet sister at the pianoforte. Now THAT was unbearable."

"Appalling. And the whole family staying behind quite until sunrise! I thought they would never leave this morning!" Louisa sighed. Bingley kept a stolid silence.

"Do you know," Caroline continued, "that the tallest one, the one named Lydia I believe, actually came and talked to me, quite impudently, as if we were the closest of friends, and rattled away about how much Miss Eliza Bennet was in love with that Wickham officer? I recall the name, isn't he the son of your former Steward, Mr. Darcy?"

"Yes, I believe that's the man," I said very shortly, turning away to conceal my anger.

"And didn't you tell me, brother, that he was quite a rascal? Certainly, even *fine eyes* love a redcoat these days…"

I wanted to punch her.

"What a family! Poor Miss Jane Bennet. Would that we could help improve her family…" Caroline shook her head, in mock pity for the Bennets.

Charles had turned crimson. I remembered then how Sir William Lucas had thrown about gross hints about upcoming nuptials between Bingley and Miss Bennet. This had gone too far. I decided to put an end to all this foolishness. His foolishness, and mine. For despite my initial certainty at being in no danger at all regarding emotional entanglement with a woman of mediocre standing, I felt that perhaps my reason was losing ground and my heart was putting forth its own reasons.

We had to leave Hertfordshire. Leave it immediately. Leave it permanently.

Georgiana Darcy

Pemberley, November 28

Today I did something quite reprehensible, yet so instructive! Mrs. Prescott came to Pemberley last week and is staying for a fortnight. Since she is Mrs. Annesley's cousin and they were brought up together, they are as thick as thieves and spend a lot of time conversing, far away (or so they think) from my tender ears. Mrs. Prescott has been a midwife for many years and usually has plenty of gossip from neighboring families to relate to her cousin. I rather enjoy Mrs. Prescott's visits because Mrs. Annesley relaxes her surveillance upon *me* then, and I savor the freedom.

I did not mean to eavesdrop, but I had run out of thread wax and instead of bothering servants, three of whom are ill with colds, I had gone down to the office in search for some, when I heard low voices and conspiratorial tones. I padded softly and stayed out of sight by the door. I had missed the earlier part of their conversation, but their exchange continued thus:

"…inconceivable that nobody ever noticed. In all my years of delivering babies into this world, I have never seen two blue-eyed parents produce a dark-eyed child."

"Is it *quite* impossible, cousin?" Mrs. Annesley asked.

"I can't say. I can only attest to my experience. And there is a resemblance about the forehead, the jaw in those young men. Old Mr. Darcy had that strong jaw."

There was a silence as they sipped their tea. Presently Mrs. Annesley spoke again.

"Perhaps people did notice, cousin, but what could anyone have said?"

The two women sighed in unison.

"Poor Lady Anne," said Mrs. Prescott. "After what she endured, after birthing Master Fitzwilliam nearly killed her, it's a miracle that our dear Georgiana ever came to be. And the three boys before him, who didn't live. And you know, after that, I told her she must not ever again…it was too dangerous, and Mr. Darcy knew it…"

Mrs. Annesley interrupted her. "Perhaps, precisely, Georgiana came to be, because Lady Anne knew about…had noticed…the resemblance. And she couldn't bear the thought of it happening again with another, and so she allowed, perhaps persuaded…old Mr. Darcy again to…" Her voice trailed, but I had a fairly good idea of what she was trying to say.

"And poor Mrs. Wickham," Mrs. Prescott said. "So slight, so frail. The baby so big. I did what I could… She knew she was not going to survive, but she was happy…she had had a son…and she said to me…"

Here Mrs. Prescott's voice became an inaudible whisper.

"Men!" Mrs. Annesley exclaimed in a bitter tone. "All the same, be they lords or ruffians. Beasts. Why couldn't he just leave her alone! Just go to town and find what he needed there… And do you think old Wickham ever knew…"

There was more whispering and then a long silence. I hardly dared to breathe. I was afraid that they could hear the beating of my heart knocking about in my chest.

Presently Mrs. Prescott spoke again. "In any case, Mrs. Younge informed me that George Wickham is now well situated, and I hope he will prosper now that he's joined the militia."

At this point, I heard Janey coming down the stairs, and I pretended I had just arrived there myself, and I asked her for the wax, quite matter-of-factly.

I returned to my room, all but suffocating. They knew! Mrs. Prescott and Mrs. Annesley had known all these years. George was not lying. He had learned the truth about his birth, and he had told me the truth.

He is my half-brother. He and Willy are half-brothers. My father… Mrs. Wickham… No wonder my father took such a great interest in George all those years.

Oh Lord, give me guidance! Now that I know for sure, what do I do? Definitely, I MUST go to Netherfield and force my brother to listen! But how?

Fitzwilliam Darcy

London, December 7

The days are short, bitter cold, and dark. We went to see *"She Stoops to Conquer"* last night. Admirably played, and despite my mediocre humor these days, I enjoyed it. But throughout, all I could think of was how Miss Elizabeth Bennet would have smiled and laughed at the hapless hero's antics. How her eyes would have sparkled. I wanted to hear her views on the premise and conclusion of the play. I found it difficult to converse with my party, who were spouting platitudes, and I probably passed for an oaf, again.

We left Netherfield a fortnight ago, and still my imagination conjures up Miss Eliza. And Caroline's assertion that she is "quite in love with Wickham" poisons my peace.

This is ridiculous. It shall soon pass.

Georgiana Darcy

Pemberley, December 8

I am so ashamed of myself I am crying hot tears tonight.

I failed in my plan to abscond. For the last few weeks, I have been gathering money for the journey, reserving a good portion of what my brother allows for my alms-giving. I have been feeling wicked for cheating the less fortunate in order to pursue my mission to Netherfield to save George. I have felt torn between two duties, and perhaps that is what shredded my courage this afternoon.

I had taken the opportunity of Mrs. Annesley being very ill to persuade Mrs. Reynolds that I could go with Janey instead, in my weekly visit to the poor. Well, we made it as far as Lambton on foot. Janey was surprised, since that is not at all my usual round. She started to ask questions. Why were we going so far? Why today, when it was so cold and windy? I told her to hush.

Shortly before we reached Lambton, it started to snow. In the village, we took refuge in the inn. I knew there was a conveyance I could hire to take me to Leicester. From there, I would surely find my way to Meryton; after all, it was closer than London. It might take a long time, but my purse was full, and although my plan was not very well formulated and I was terrified of all the ills that might befall us, I kept telling myself not to be such a coward.

My inquiries were met with high suspicion—of course, everyone knows Miss Darcy, and what on earth could she be doing, rambling about without a suitable companion in the dark days of winter, inquiring about going to Leicester? And there was indeed a coach to Leicester, but it would be later in the afternoon, and the coachman was grumbling about the weather making roads impassable if the blizzard continued. I watched the snow, which was falling thickly now, and I lost heart. We found a conveyance back to Pemberley. Mrs. Reynolds was very upset by our long absence. I told her a pack of wicked but plausible lies with the straightest of faces. I am an excellent dissimulator. And I had given Janey a nice present to make sure she did not tell anyone anything. How useful money is sometimes!

Now, sitting in my chamber, watching the frozen, white landscape, I realize that what I attempted was impossible. And it was very foolish of me to think I could use Janey as a companion in such a journey. And very wrong, trying to use her in this manner. I am a fool, but really, I failed only because I am a girl. Had I been a boy, this would have been easy. But I am not a boy.

I failed, I failed! What will become of George?

Fitzwilliam Darcy

London, December 9

I congratulate myself more than ever on having sought out a close acquaintance with Captain Pratt; and I am fortunate that he is a skillful and faithful spy. He has succeeded in forming a solid friendship with Wickham. Together they are often invited to Longbourn. I have asked Pratt to report in the utmost detail on Wickham's movements, nothing more; he has no idea that I nurture a kind of *penchant* toward Eliza Bennet; still, he singled her out in his letter, writing that she seemed "quite taken with Wickham, who it must be said has engaging manners and is becoming a favorite among the gentler sex in town." So. Caroline was not lying. Quite taken with Wickham, indeed. I thought she might have better taste. This makes me unaccountably angry. Why was I not able to stir similar sentiments in her? Why do inferior men succccd whcrc I fail?

But why should I care? An alliance with Miss Eliza Bennet is unthinkable.

Pratt also mentions that the town is astir with the news that Mr. Collins, my aunt's pretentious protégé, proposed to Miss Eliza, that she refused him, and that her friend Miss Lucas swiftly replaced Eliza in the man's matrimonial quest. So, poor Miss Lucas and the clerical stooge are engaged. I must say I feel some relief, knowing that neither Miss Bennet nor Miss Eliza Bennet is to be sacrificed to the future heir of Longbourn. I am not at all surprised that Eliza refused the offer; it is unthinkable to imagine her coupled with that obsequious cleric. I do feel a bit sorry for Miss Lucas. She will have to deal with my aunt Catherine at Hunsford, and I fear Miss Lucas will be completely subjugated. Had it been Miss Eliza Bennet, I am certain she would have had enough pluck to stand up to Her Ladyship. It might have been rather entertaining.

Well, there I go, thinking of her again. I have to be honest. When I read that Eliza had refused the pompous fool, my heart leapt with joy.

I need a distraction.

I will send for my sister as soon as possible.

Georgiana Darcy

Pemberley, December 15

Well, it's a good thing I did not proceed with my plan to go to Netherfield, since they all left for town at the end of November. It is strange that my brother did not write me for such a long time to inform me of this. The letter I received today was the first in almost two weeks. And I have not heard a word from George. I suppose George was not able to meet with Willy at all. I wonder if his letters have been intercepted. Perhaps he is very busy soldiering.

Despite my misery at the uncertainty, there is great joy in my heart, for tomorrow Mrs. Annesley and I depart for town, as my brother has decided that I will spend Christmas with him. The Bingleys will be there too. I am certain I will have the opportunity to talk to Willy about George. The difficulty will lie in bringing him to accept the truth. I will have to use diplomatic skills to rival those of our great Queen Elizabeth.

And then of course, there will be the puzzle of how we shall all behave together once the fences are mended. As a family? Given the resentment that occurred on both sides, that is not very likely. How did families deal with such situations in the past? For I am sure ours is not the first case. Shocking, yes, but not unique. I have read enough novels to know that strange things happen in every family! I wish I could talk to someone I can trust. Despite my discovery of a second brother, I feel more than ever the burden of loneliness. And I am certain that Willy feels lonely too. I will be so happy to see him, and I am so eager, wild really, to be among company again!

PART II

Fitzwilliam Darcy

London, December 26

I have been remiss in putting my thoughts down on paper. We have been very busy, and it is all for the best, to avoid unpleasant thoughts or all-too-pleasant but dangerous reveries. But a few things have happened that I must faithfully record.

Charles and I took a walk on a frosty day last week, away from prying eyes and eager ears. He confessed to me that his heart was still in Hertfordshire and that he could not forget Miss Bennet as I had instructed him to do.

I am quite the villain, for almost as soon as we were settled in town, I went to work on him and his sentiments at every opportunity, when I should have been disciplining myself instead.

I tried not to be brutal about it. In fact, Caroline had actually laid the groundwork by mentioning in her falsely understated way, a few days after we had left Netherfield, that letters she had received from an acquaintance in Meryton indicated that "officers were continuously going in and out of Longbourn and that *ALL* of the Miss Bennets were quite enamored."

Bingley's face fell so visibly when she related this intelligence that I felt sorry for him.

"Yes, dear brother," Caroline continued. "Even the angelic Miss Jane Bennet can have her head turned by a redcoat; you know she is very likely to attract an officer and possibly receive an offer at any time. That would be very appropriate for her station in life."

I said nothing, but on our walk a few days later, Bingley applied to me, saying he was longing to return to Netherfield, or at least to write to Miss Bennet, and he asked what I thought of this project.

"Well, it would be rather forward of you to write to her. But I am not one to speculate on such matters."

"But did you not think she had some partiality toward me?" he asked, his eyes rather anxious.

"Charles, to be quite honest, her staid countenance indicated to me at all times that she seemed pleased with your attentions toward her but not at all enamored. If you recall, her mother once mentioned a gentleman quite in love with her, who was unable to stir up any emotion. She may be what they call an ice queen. She has been blessed with very good looks and knows her power over men, and perhaps toys with them."

"I can't believe that, Darcy! She spoke and conversed with animation and enjoyment with me, and sincerely, as far as I could tell," Bingley replied, "and she seemed very far from being such a virago as what you describe. Our tastes and ideas converged so perfectly…"

"My dear friend, women are enigmas. They often act in such a way as to make you believe what is not true, and make you not believe what is, and it is best not to rely on one's own judgment in such cases, but to defer to friends' advice. The fish in the fishbowl is a poor judge of the other fish that are in the fishbowl."

He looked at me quizzically. This may not have been my most felicitous speech.

"I mean that I witnessed not one sign of deep emotion in Miss Bennet's regard for you. I am sure she considers you a pleasant man, and those poor girls were desperate for partners at their dances. Of course she smiled at you."

Bingley sighed deeply and was quiet a long time. He looked so unhappy that I was starting to feel ashamed of myself. I was almost ready to blurt out something that would give him hope—or at least inflict less pain—but I reminded myself that prudence was of the essence in this situation.

After we returned home, as we were warming our hands by the fire, he said finally, "Darcy, there is no remedy. You saw the many young ladies that we have been in company with in the last couple of weeks… Well, I find them insufferable. My thoughts go back to Miss Bennet, every day, every night."

"Please, my friend, do spare me such details as your nocturnal thoughts," I said, trying for a bit of humor. Judging from his expression, I failed. "Come, do not be despondent. There are plenty of lovely ladies in town, and perhaps one will strike your fancy. And do not torture yourself over something that may not exist. In fact, what Captain Pratt has written to me corroborates what Caroline said last week. Be aware that the Bennet family is entertaining officers at their home for teas, dinners, suppers, impromptu dances… She has probably forgotten you already."

Bingley was quiet again. He soon retired for the night, and I poked at the fire rather violently.

Georgiana Darcy

London, December 29

I was expecting to have a whirlwind of a time here in Town, but that has not been the case. In fact, my life is not much different from being at Pemberley, except that we have been to the theater three times, and Willy and Charles Bingley are here, although they are out much of the time. At least I have the relief of not seeing Mr. Bingley's sisters too much, for they are staying in Mr. Hurst's home two miles from here. They call often, but they do not stay long, and I do not have to suffer their daily intimacy as I did at Pemberley last summer. They are boring and fawning, and I hate being the object of their solicitude and advice.

Mr. Hudson has been retained to instruct me at the pianoforte, and I am quite happy to be guided by such a capable musician. Unlike my previous instructor, Mr. Hudson is rather young, perhaps a few years older than Willy, and he is handsome and kind. And what a virtuoso at the keyboard! I love to see his hands fly over the keys, and I redouble my efforts and practice many hours daily.

Willy is pleased by my zeal, I can tell from his smiles, and often I glance up from a particularly difficult piece and see him looking at me with infinite fondness. He is the best of brothers, and as I write this, I recall that now I must use the word in the plural at all times in my mind. My brothers. How different my life would have been if the truth had been known to me from the beginning!

But how best to broach the topic of George's relation to us? The problem with being here, of course, is that I cannot receive letters from George. I suppose he is still in Meryton. I feel anxious and jittery, and I have not worked up the courage to talk to Willy yet. I know that if I blurt the truth out without having a strategy in place, Willy will not accept it, might think me quite mad, send me back to Pemberley, and all will be ruined. I must be artful, strategic, quite Napoleonic in my approach! So, I mull it over, and over, and over, and often I get discouraged, so I play and practice. Music helps my brain forget. I wish life had the notes written out in a score, it would be so much easier.

Fitzwilliam Darcy

London, December 30

Five years ago today, my father died. I am a bit despondent, as usual on this sad anniversary. Every year for four years, on this day I have recalled our last serious talk, about a week before he passed. His ardent hope was that I would be the best master that Pemberley had ever had. He said he had done many wrongs. He told me to be careful. He said that the most important task for me was to marry well.

"Marry well? You mean…a wealthy woman?" I asked.

The pain and illness had carved his features taut, but he smiled.

"Does Pemberley seem poor to you…in need of gold?"

"Indeed not."

"Then…" He shook his head. "Marry well, and take care of Georgiana, my little angel."

"Of course, please do not worry on that account. You know I love Georgiana more than anything."

He seemed pleased with my response. He closed his eyes, and very slowly said:

"So. Three things. Marry well. Georgiana. And be mindful of my godson."

"You have my word. But, please, in what way should I marry well? What do you mean?"

He shook a bit, as if laughing inside, and he opened his eyes. Was that a twinkle of amusement or a shard of pain that I saw in his dark eyes?

"Be truthful to yourself. You will know."

After that conversation, he turned worse. He became incoherent. He requested several times to be taken to the hunting lodge—an abandoned cottage on the estate. Of course, with the brutal winter weather, we were not going to indulge this whim and move him from his warm bed.

Within two days, he was no longer speaking. Within a week, he was dead.

I rehearse this last exchange all too often, and I seek to understand what he was trying to convey to me. I feel that I am missing something—everything.

Of the three paternal directives, I have failed at every one. Firstly, I have not yet married, well or otherwise; I am not at all certain that I "will know," as Father claimed I would.

Secondly, Georgiana. I take care of her as well as I can, but she is a young woman now, and I am confused by such creatures. Her running away to meet George at Ramsgate last spring pierced me like a dagger. It skewered my innards. I was never able to understand her garbled explanation…of course, she was young and confused, what can she know about rakes? And her talk of loving him… It was more than I could bear. I sent her instantly back to Pemberley. I dismissed Mrs. Younge without references. Had that duplicitous woman been a man, I would have thrashed her. I refused to listen to her incoherent ramblings.

And thirdly, of course, my father's "godson." How can I abide by my father's two last wishes when they contradict each other? When taking care of Georgiana means banishing George, whom I promised to be mindful of? But what did "be mindful of" mean? Did my father see that George was an unpromising young man? Did he mean for me to be on my guard against him, when I had always thought he meant that I should be as generous as possible with him, as per the terms of his will? Did he find something out about George before dying, something he was unable to communicate to me due to his illness?

Now I know that George is a scoundrel. Therefore, I think I can safely cross George off my list without thinking that I am betraying my father's last wishes. So, next, it is imperative that I see what I can do about Georgiana. She seems agitated at times, and at others she seems wistful, occasionally listless. She is seventeen. It's a difficult age. She complained of being lonely at Pemberley. Perhaps I should let her move in society a little more. I wonder how she feels about Charles Bingley. I must at least test the waters before the year is out. Which gives me exactly one day.

Georgiana Darcy

London, January 1, the First Hours of the New Year

What a strange day yesterday—yesteryear—was.

First, I have to say I am brimming with impatience! Fitzy is coming tomorrow, no, that would be today, as the clock struck midnight about an hour ago.

This is the best news I have received since I've been in town. It seems Willy is always more cheerful when our cousin is here, and Fitzy is one of the few persons who can crack Willy's strange armor of—I don't know what—a diffidence, a complication where things should be easy.

Fitzy's presence is all the more desirable as yesterday, Willy talked about important things indeed! And I hoped this would be my best chance to broach the subject of George. But instead, this is what happened. I think I can recall very faithfully how our conversation went.

We were alone in the drawing room, the hour was drawing late, and Charles had already retired for the night, pretexting great fatigue, and Willy, who had been indulging in a bit of wine, asked me to stay a bit and ring in the new year with him.

Rather abruptly, he asked if I minded that Charles Bingley was so constantly with us in the house.

"No, of course not. Mr. Bingley is always pleasant."

"Do you find him very…agreeable…in every way?" he asked a bit hesitantly.

I perceived what his meaning was. I couldn't help laughing.

"Brother, do you mean to ask me if I am in love with him?"

He made that funny face he makes when he is taken aback. I love it.

"Well. Are you?"

"Oh, I assure you I am not! I love him dearly, but as *your* friend; or maybe more as an uncle. And less than Cousin Fitzwilliam. Were you thinking I should…what, marry him?"

"Well, no, not necessarily… I was just wondering… You are coming of age… Young women have fancies…"

I was afraid he was going to refer to what happened at Ramsgate. It was time to deflect.

"Willy, I could ask *you* if you find his sister Caroline very agreeable. What would you say to that?" I asked, thinking his question had given me the right to tease him a bit.

He colored. "Good God! No! That is, she is a…a fine woman, and my good friend's sister, but she is not…"

I thought now that his confusion might give me an opening. I felt for the first time that I was not just a little child in his eyes. He had asked me if I was in love with Mr. Bingley! Though the particular choice of this possible mate struck me as singular, the idea of my rising to such stature seemed to give me some power. At least, so I thought at first.

"My dear brother, I am teasing you. I assure you I really want a little more time. I seek to know myself better before I…that is, I would say that right now I would be more desirous of having a sister than of marrying. Would it have been different for *you* if *you* had had…a brother…for instance, wouldn't you be happy if you were, perhaps, let's say, to find, maybe, a long-lost brother?"

He looked at me quizzically. Given my incoherence, that was not surprising.

"I mean, haven't you been lonely, growing up without a brother?"

He paused a moment. Instead of answering my question, he threw it back at me.

"You mean to say that you have been lonely growing up without a sister."

I inclined my head a bit to the side, to indicate acquiescence, although that was not my point. I wanted to introduce the topic of George, not mope about myself. He took both my hands in his.

"My dear Georgiana, I thought that might be the case."

To my dismay, instead of allowing me to pursue the case of HIS needing to find out that he already HAD a brother, and to let him know clearly that an elopement was not on my mind when George and I were caught by him at Ramsgate, that I was not an overly nubile female that needed to be mated as soon as possible, Willy, I believe, caught the notion that I was eager for *him* to marry. And he embarked on a disquisition on why it was incumbent on him to marry soon: heirs, Pemberley, Derbyshire, England, and God save the King…

"So," he said after rather a lengthy speech on these topics, "in this matter, I do seek your advice, Georgiana."

I was flabbergasted. My advice. This was novel indeed.

"What would *you* like in a sister, Georgiana? What qualities, what personality would make *you* happy in a sister?"

I did not have to spend much time on thinking of my answer, as all my life I have created in my head my ideal sister. So I took the plunge, knowing this would probably not be what he sought in a wife, and curious to see his reaction. "Well, she must be…real. Authentic. Free of artifice. Are there such women in London?" I asked with a smile.

He smiled back. "I am not certain of it. What do you mean by real and authentic?"

"Lively. Not too guarded. Frank. Outspoken. Not one who so much fears to offend that you don't ever know what she is thinking."

He smiled again. "Anything else?"

"I would want my sister to be playful. But intelligent. And informed, of course, not a simpleton. I suppose she would have to have the usual accomplishments, to fit in society. Although I would be quite jealous if she outshone me on the pianoforte."

He nodded. He looked at once very serious and amazed, and extremely attentive to what I was saying. I was starting to think this was the oddest conversation we had ever had.

"And handsome, of course. Or at least…not a horseface, brother, for pity's sake."

"A horseface?" He looked astonished.

"Like Miss Amanda Edwards."

He laughed heartily. This was going well. He does not laugh often, these days. Then, he guzzled the last of his port. His cheeks had turned rather pink, on account of the wine, I think. Then, he looked very earnestly into my eyes.

"And what if in addition to all that, she was in fact very pretty, and she liked to…to run?"

"To run? You mean, outside?"

"Yes. In woods, or fields, in sunshine and rain…"

"Then she would be absolutely perfect, my dear brother." I said laughingly.

The clock struck twelve. He kissed me and hugged me.

"Happy new year, Georgiana."

"Happy new year to you, Willy!"

Fitzwilliam Darcy

London, January 6

I did not write for a whole week. My cousin being here has allowed me to start the new year on such a positive note, I frankly have not felt the need to tame my demons through my pen. His rational and cheerful manner, coupled with that of Bingley, means that our dinner conversations are always lively and well-informed, and I can tell by Georgiana's smiles and serene countenance that she enjoys our quiet revelries too. She is becoming less shy about performing on the pianoforte before company. She is gaining assurance and poise every day.

I have been mulling over whether my conversation with Georgiana about her "ideal sister" on New Year's Eve was a wise thing. I had overindulged in the drink, and talking to her made me happier at the time. I was so overjoyed at her description matching point for point Miss Eliza Bennet—including the lady's skills not surpassing hers at the piano—that I found it difficult to keep a stony face. Georgiana looked so radiant when I spoke to her. Perhaps I have been too circumspect all my life. Perhaps Georgiana craves more openness from me. She seemed so content at seeing me so—dare I say—happy…? But how did I allow myself to hope that night, when all reports indicate that Miss Eliza Bennet, whom I could never marry anyway, if only on account of her intolerable mother, is in love with none other than George Wickham?

The next day, I berated myself for having overstepped my boundaries in several respects with Georgiana, but after a week's cogitations on the matter and my last few conversations with my cousin, I think it might not have been such a mistake after all. Somehow, Fitzy (here I go calling James "Fitzy," as Georgiana does) has a way of smoothing over objections and casting light on murky areas.

Yesterday, as the day was unexpectedly fine, he invited me to stroll along the boulevard with him. He seemed to have something on his mind, and indeed he did.

"Darcy, you do realize that you, unlike me, are the master of your own destiny, I hope?" he said as soon as we had descended to the street. He was referring to a previous conversation during which I had bemoaned the stern dictum of society regarding marriage.

"We none of us are masters of our destiny, cousin."

"Aye, but you at least may marry whomever you choose."

"You are mistaken. I cannot. I cannot be blind to the necessity I am under to choose a gentlewoman. A woman of consequence and high breeding. Nothing less will do to avoid our Aunt Catherine's wrath!" I said, half-jokingly, half-bitterly.

"Are you telling me you prefer to please that pretentious, imperious, snobbish woman than yourself? In a matter as important as the woman who will share your life and your bed and bear your children, you take orders from Aunt Catherine?"

"When you put it in that light, it does sound ridiculous."

"Because it *is* ridiculous. *She* is ridiculous. If you were so keen to please our aunt, you should have proposed to little Anne five years ago, when you came of age." He smiled broadly.

"You know *that* will never happen," I said, returning his smile.

"Very true. It would be cruel. Anne has actually confided in me that she has no interest in marrying you or any other man."

"Indeed?" I was wondering how the Colonel was able to draw such information out of the most reticent people. A talent I clearly do not possess.

"She told me she wished she could turn Popish and escape to a convent in Italy."

"I suppose we cannot blame her, given the mother."

"Since Miss de Bourgh is out of the question, I have the feeling you have someone in mind who is her very opposite. Now, do not be alarmed, but yesterday I had an interesting conversation with Georgiana, who mentioned—"

"Georgiana?"

"—that you may have discovered a very pretty woman who likes to run."

I stopped and turned to face James. The colonel's smile was ironic, but his eyes were warm. I did not know how to reply. Georgiana had betrayed me— well, it is true I had not asked her for any secrecy. My own damned fault for getting tipsy… I felt hot in the face.

"Well, Darcy? Come, out with it! Is she a commoner then?"

"Not exactly. Her father is a gentleman. But I believe their financial situation is not satisfactory."

"Ah, yes, financial situations. And her mother?"

I let out an exasperated sigh. "Excruciatingly vulgar."

"Ah. But the young woman herself?"

"Excruciatingly beautiful, well-informed, eloquent, charming, accomplished—"

"My dear Darcy, I do believe you are in love," the Colonel said in a subdued but jubilating tone.

"And *she* too is in love—with another man," I said. It was difficult for me to keep my tone even.

"Oh. I see. Do you know the inconvenient fellow?"

"Too well." I really did not want to talk about Wickham as my rival. I had told James all about what had happened at Ramsgate shortly after the event took place. My heart was burning with indignation just thinking about it.

"So, it is hopeless?"

"It would have been hopeless anyway. How can I marry a woman whose mother is an insult to the female species? A monstrous incarnation of the fair sex?"

"My dear Darcy, what an interesting question! I shall have an answer for you no later than this evening. I will enroll Georgiana's help to tease this puzzle out."

"I implore you to leave my sister out of this."

"And I will do no such thing. Come, the light is waning, and I am wanting my tea."

Georgiana Darcy

London, January 7

I will be very upset to see Fitzy leave the day after tomorrow. However, perhaps his absence will give me more time alone with Willy, so I can broach the subject of George. I thought of confiding to Fitzy, but Willy would be impossibly angry if he ever learned that I talked to his cousin before I informed *him* of this whole affair.

Yesterday we had another very strange conversation. Mr. Bingley was out with his sisters, so it was just my brother, my cousin, and myself in the drawing room.

"Georgiana, your brother posed a question that has me tied up in knots. We appeal to your judgment as an accomplished and well-read young lady to set it right."

"Cousin, you are treading thin ice…" my brother began.

"The question is this: how can a man marry a woman whose mother is a monster?"

"A monster? What sort of monster?" I asked, a little surprised at the silliness of this question.

"Darcy? What sort of monster?" Fitzy asked in his comical, falsely serious way. My brother looked at us both in turn and then shook his head and smiled.

"I see I am outnumbered. All right, then. A monster of a mother, who interrupts, upbraids, self-congratulates, whines, cavils, complains, or, when it serves her better, is intolerably obsequious."

"Is that all, Darcy?"

"Has a loud voice, shrewish eyes, a stentorian cackle, but believes herself most polite, most genteel."

"Ah!" I exclaimed. "I see! You gentlemen are referring to Aunt Catherine! Has my cousin Anne found a suitor?"

I saw Willy staring at the Colonel, who stared back at him. They looked shocked. You could have heard a pin drop.

"Why are you both so surprised? You didn't think I would guess so fast?" I asked. They looked unaccountably taken aback.

"It is not Lady Catherine," my brother said slowly.

"It certainly sounds like her," I said. I noticed that Fitzy was repressing laughter now.

"The monster in question does not have the *fortune* of Lady Catherine," he said. "So, Darcy, here's the rub. A monstrous mother *with money* is a respectable person, and all bow to her; even her nephews afford her respect, and her sickly daughter is highly marriageable. However, the same sort of monstrous mother, but *without money*, is a vulgar, detestable character, and *her* beautiful and healthy daughter must confine herself to ruffians or resign herself to old-maidenhood. So, Georgiana, can you answer the question that was posed, with all the seriousness you can muster: How can a man marry the daughter of a monster?"

"I suppose daughters are not necessarily identical to their mothers. Certainly my cousin Anne is nothing like Aunt Catherine. If the man likes the daughter but not the mother, the best course of action would be for the man to stay far away from the mother, once he has secured the hand of the daughter."

"Brilliantly reasoned, Miss Darcy," Fitzy said, bowing theatrically before me. Willy and I both laughed. "Mr. Darcy, I hope you are satisfied."

The rest of the evening, I asked in vain what this quizzing was about, but Fitzy would just laugh and dismiss my questions, while my brother simply smiled and shook his head, muttering under his breath something about officious colonels. But there was a very unusual softness about his eyes the rest of the evening.

So, since it is not my Aunt Catherine that is the monster (although she *is* an ogress), I believe they were referring to someone else. Perhaps the lady who likes to run and is very pretty has an obnoxious mother.

Fitzwilliam Darcy

London, January 28

I did something today that I am not very proud of, but which was necessary. Actually, it is not something I did, but something I did not do. Sins of omission cannot be as brutal as those of commission, perhaps?

I did not tell Bingley that Miss Bennet was in town. Caroline, catching me alone, informed me of the fact, told me that she had visited Miss Bennet in a less-than-elegant dwelling in Cheapside, and that the lady was as serene as ever and did not evince the slightest interest in meeting again with Charles.

Though I am not sure she was perfectly truthful, I will take that assertion at face value. It is best that I not inform Charles about Miss Bennet's presence here. There is no need to revive an affection that would go nowhere. Charles has not brought up the subject since our last talk on the topic, when I convinced him that Miss Bennet's social life now included other men. Therefore, he may have quite forgotten her.

Winter rages on, cold, harsh, dark. We go to the theater quite often. Georgiana comes with us only occasionally; after mulling it over, I had rather she didn't expose herself excessively to the world just yet. She is diligently working to perfect her accomplishments. But when she sings at the pianoforte, I cannot help but recall Miss Eliza's sultry, enchanting voice. I feel a dark rage when I think that she may be singing thus in front of officers. In front of Wickham.

Would that this winter would be over soon!

February 20

The days are finally starting to lengthen and soften a bit, and with a rather sunny and mild morning came a letter from Captain Pratt. It had been misdirected and thus took longer to reach me than I would have liked. But the ray of sunshine it brought to my soul is undeniable.

Pratt writes that despite the appearance of partiality that he had observed between Wickham and Elizabeth Bennet, the rogue is now paying court to another young lady, a certain Miss King, who has recently inherited a fortune large enough to tempt him, and they are engaged.

More importantly, Pratt unwittingly provides information that he did not know I desired. He still enjoys invitations to Longbourn with other officers, though less often than before Christmas. On the news of Wickham's new object, he describes only the younger two Bennet sisters as being brokenhearted:

"The eldest sister is in London, as you might know, and Elizabeth Bennet is as cheerful and cordial as ever now that Wickham has found other pursuits. It seems Wickham was not such a great favorite of hers after all, as last evening, when the youngest sister, Lydia, literally sobbed at the news of Wickham's engagement to Miss King, Miss E. Bennet lectured Lydia on the silliness of her behavior. Miss E. seemed somewhat relieved to be free of Wickham's company. I had noticed a certain distancing from him on her part in the last month, even when he was rather assiduous toward her. And that, Sir, is all the news I can relate regarding Mr. Wickham, except that there are increasing rumors of his unpaid debts among certain tradesmen in Meryton. I suspect Miss King will be immensely helpful in that respect."

So, not only is Wickham out of the way for good, it seems he never really had any standing as a rival. How I tortured myself with that thought! All for nothing, as it turns out. The fact that she does not pine for Wickham lifts Eliza's stature in my regard. May I allow myself to dream?

Perhaps I should take Georgiana's advice on how a man can marry a woman with a monster for a mother. Secure the daughter, and then, stay far away… But how to secure the daughter? And is this a good choice? I must be vigilant regarding my feelings. Was I bewitched by Miss Eliza, was this a temporary infatuation? Will my regard stand the test of time? How might I ever determine this?

February 28

Another strange coincidence, and again my heart rejoices! Aunt Catherine may be, for once, very obliging in serving my purposes. I just received a letter, which, after the usual panegyric of Anne (and herself), continues thus:

"Mrs. Collins tells me she is to have company soon, for in addition to her father and sister, she has invited a friend from Longbourn. The woman is Mr. Collins's cousin (I believe she is the next-to-oldest of the Bennet sisters) and

will be her guest at Hunsford for an indefinite period. They are to arrive in a few days. Although I am used to loftier company, it will not be beneath me to receive them all at Rosings. I daresay the young ladies will never have seen a more imposing edifice, or a more sumptuous interior. You should know I had the small breakfast room redone in red and gold velvet, with tasteful green satin for the draperies and wainscoting in an aubergine shade. I had to constantly watch the artisans at work, but thanks to my zealous guidance, the result is a pleasure to behold. Mrs. Jenkins exclaims upon its beauties daily. The guests will no doubt voice their amazement at the splendors of the park and the perfection of my table. I often see the most astonished and grateful expressions among those who exist under penurious circumstances and never had a French meal in their life, when they are allowed to sample the exquisite morsels of sustenance at Rosings.

"We have been very dull here for several months. Anne is in rather indifferent health, but after such a winter, who is not? She will rally in the spring. Perhaps she will like the company of girls her age. Indeed, I expect you and Colonel Fitzwilliam to be my guests for Easter. It has been a long time since you visited, despite my many invitations, and..."

She goes on in her usual way. Oh yes, Aunt Catherine, we (or at least I) shall perhaps condescend to stay at Rosings for a spell. And enjoy the company of the guests at the parsonage. Perhaps I will find that my *engouement* for Miss Eliza was just a passing fancy; and if so, this torture will abate. Life will be as it was before.

London, March 3

This torture will abate! A passing fancy! Hah! I am the greatest of fools.

I still have trouble believing what happened last night.

Since most of our acquaintance have come down with colds, last night it was just Colonel Fitzwilliam and I going to Drury Lane. He has been impatient to see Edmund Kean in the role of *Coriolanus*, and to tell the truth, his enthusiasm bubbled over onto me. Before setting off for the theatre, we spent a good deal of time discussing our hopes for a good production of this play. He was quite justifiably amazed then, when shortly after entering the theater, I turned on my heel and headed back outside.

Miss Bennet and Miss Eliza Bennet were there. They were sitting with a fashionable-looking woman. I am quite sure that they did not see me. Miss Bennet was as handsome as ever, but Miss Eliza was even more exquisite than I remembered. She was wearing a simple light blue gown with white fur trim, her bright chestnut hair was dressed in a riot of curls that reminded me of a certain muddy-day event, and she was talking animatedly with the fashionable lady. In this worldly setting, she looked quite at ease, quite unbothered by the finery and artifice surrounding her. I felt a jolt. The same unconquerable feeling of desire and admiration I had experienced before jarred all my senses and rendered me incapable of coherent speech and action.

"Darcy, what on earth are you doing?" the colonel asked, following me as I hurried outside.

"I am unwell. So sorry." I talked breathlessly. "It came suddenly. Damned headache, pounding. Intolerable. Must be that cold everyone else has. You stay and enjoy the play. You can relate the details to me later. I must go to bed."

The colonel looked concerned and perhaps a bit dubious. He knows I have a strong constitution and am rarely ill. I was able to convince him to go back in, and I headed home, where, thank goodness, I was able to reach my chamber without too much notice. I sent Carruthers away. I swallowed a long draught of cold water, and then something a little stronger. I was fairly shaking.

And all night, all I could think of was her. Seeing her at Rosings.

There is no doubt in my mind that the infatuation is far from over.

London, March 15

Another letter from my aunt. Perhaps it might contain news of Miss Elizabeth Bennet, I thought as I broke the seal. I also hoped the letter would contain information that would discourage my ardor. It did not. It did occasionally provoke frank laughter on my part though—and also, ironically, it clarified my feelings. After her usual vapid pieces of gossip, Lady Catherine writes:

"The lady friend of Mrs. Collins is in fact the young woman who refused Mr. Collins's offer of marriage. Although this was a stupid thing for her to do, given the entailment of her father's estate and the inevitable plummeting into destitution that this will cause for all the Bennet girls, I cannot but rejoice that Mrs. Collins was his final choice, for she is a far better match for my protégé. Miss Bennet has several faults, among which the greatest I believe is her lack of humility. [Oh yes, dear Aunt, you are a specialist in humility!] *Unlike your cousin Anne, whose quiet demeanor is much to be admired in a woman,* [hah, think I… Anne is more to be pitied than admired…and perhaps, dear Aunt, you should follow your own advice!] *this Miss Elizabeth Bennet is very forward, shockingly outspoken, far too frank. And another deplorable thing, which I heard from Mrs. Jenkins, is that she has been seen sauntering about in*

the wooded lanes…quite alone. And running! Without her bonnet! [You list all the attributes that Georgiana desired in a sister…and you bring up memories in me that stir my soul… Dear God!]

"But I am satisfied to have her here. My guidance, my advice, and Anne's example will no doubt teach her a few useful object lessons [no doubt, Madam!] *for which later she will be immensely grateful,* [I think not…] *as they might secure her a prudent match. She has an acceptable countenance,* [acceptable countenance? She is the best-looking woman I have ever seen!] *and so perhaps she may thus lure a gentleman of no mean condition—if she keeps her wildness in check.* [Ah, but perhaps that wildness is precisely what might lure a gentleman…and dear Lord, am I that gentleman?]

"Dear Nephew, I can now expect your arrival in less than a fortnight. I am pleased that Colonel Fitzwilliam has obtained extended leave for a visit as well. You must relent and allow Georgiana to be among your party. As soon as the weather improves, she may walk about in the park with Anne, which no doubt will ameliorate her health and appetite. I know you are longing to see her…etc."

Indeed, I do long to see "her." And no, I still do not think Georgiana should go. I must not let Georgiana's opinion influence mine. I must decide on my own. And I must not have my sister forging bonds of friendship that might have to be severed, if I find that I have been mistaken.

Rosings, March 23

James and I arrived at Rosings this afternoon. I am glad to be finally alone in my chamber. My aunt's exclamatory effusions and vacuous declarations have worn my patience thin. Although I know it always takes me a few days to get into the habit of ignoring her, today I found it exceedingly difficult to be civil. Perhaps it is because I have another object in being here than acting the dutiful nephew, and as the moment of meeting Miss Elizabeth again is almost upon me, I begin to lose command of my emotions.

On our journey, James was not duped by my efforts to hide my impatience.

"Darcy, you are rarely this excited at the prospect of visiting Rosings! Why the rush? Why couldn't we stay and enjoy that enticing mince pie the hosteler's wife was dangling before my hungry eyes?"

"Nothing specific, I would just like to arrive before sunset. And you had filled your belly enough. I did you a favor and spared you the ills of dyspepsia while traveling."

"Indeed, if I didn't know better, I might think Georgiana was right and Anne had found a suitor—in you."

I laughed and told him that there were actually other, perhaps more interesting persons to be met with—not exactly at Rosings, but nearby—and that I would be happy to introduce him to some acquaintances I had met in Hertfordshire. This led to a few questions from him regarding Charles. He had noticed that this winter Charles appeared less ebullient than previously and seemed almost despondent at times.

"Bingley," said I, "had some unlucky entanglements, rather like mine with Miss Amanda Edwards."

"Darcy, I told you from the very first that the woman was not worth your regard."

"Yes, I can rely on you to be lucid where I am blind. You have wizard-like talents."

"Do not give me so much power. I simply look and listen. But what happened with Bingley?"

"He was enamored of a girl whose family was truly objectionable."

"Ah, here we are again. Objectionable. By way of fortune?"

"Not so much fortune, though they are far from wealthy. No, the problem lay in their lack of propriety."

"In what way?"

"A complete disregard for decorum in society—the mother, the sisters, the father. Though the woman herself, I must say to her credit, had impeccable manners."

"Poor girl. Do you believe Bingley had serious designs on her?"

"If he did, I quite removed them. To my great satisfaction, on three counts. First, I observed the woman closely and saw that she did not return his affection to the same degree. Second, she is quite pretty and will have no lack of suitors that are a better match. Third, I will have no friend of mine reproaching me, ten years hence, that I did not warn him of the quagmire into which he was stepping."

"If she lacked affection, and her family lacked propriety, you did your friend a great service indeed."

"That is what I hope." Despite the Colonel's response being exactly what I wanted to hear, I was not quite happy with myself.

James kept quiet the rest of the way, but I was conscious of his eye on me, and just before we arrived, he made me promise that the introduction to my acquaintances would be made as soon as possible.

"Anything," said he, "to relieve us from the noise of the aunt and the silence of the cousin."

Therefore, tomorrow, to the Parsonage we shall repair. I am curious to see what the Colonel will think of Miss Eliza. I will observe them closely.

94

Georgiana

London, March 24

My wickedness knows no bounds. Not only have I been guilty of eavesdropping on conversations, but I have now also, today, actively and purposefully, broken the trust of my brother.

It's only a letter that I intercepted. Of course, I know he would be as angry as the devil if he knew what I had done. But I really believed I was doing it for his own good. The circumstances were too tempting.

I had to know who it was that kept writing to him. Ever since we have been in town together, I have seen him receive the same sorts of letters. Always a one-sheet, cross-written letter, with a wafer. He would stop whatever he was doing and open and read it immediately, unless we were in company, in which case he would hurry away with it on some pretext or other. But sometimes it was just me and him in the room, and I would observe him surreptitiously. His expression as he read was always one of great concentration, but sometimes he looked elated and sometimes his brow darkened in a terrifying way. I had to know what was causing such anguish in him. Was it a woman writing? Sometimes I feel I am indeed my brother's keeper. There is a fragility in him that he hides very well…but I am not blind to it.

So when a new maid, hesitant and scared, came into the drawing room today to ask me where she was supposed to put letters for Mister Darcy while Carruthers was away, I smiled and told her I would take care of it.

As soon as she had gone, I took my embroidery scissors and snipped the wafer.

I read the letter.

It was not from, or about, a woman. It was about George.

It seems my brother has set a spy on George. The man—I think he is a military sort and knows George very well—he says that George "is indeed set upon marrying Miss King." However, he has heard rumors that George's debts in Meryton are far more serious than what was thought at first. There are rumors of "debauchery," he writes. I do not know exactly what that word means, but it sounds awful. I suppose Miss King has not heard these malicious rumors. If she does, it is possible that she might not be so keen on having her fortune dispersed on gambling and drinking debts.

I don't believe any of it. George, a gambler and a drunk! If it is true, it can only be because he has lost all hope, because now he feels he must marry where there is no love, and all because my brother—*his half-brother*—has turned him out penniless. This cannot be allowed. I must help him. But how? I can't even talk to Willy.

I have failed. Completely failed. Again, in every circumstance, I fail. I could kick myself, for I let every opportunity to talk to Willy wither away, and now Willy and Fitzy are gone to Aunt Catherine's... I am alone here with a retinue of watchful servants and zealous tutors. Nobody can help.

Now I wish I hadn't opened this letter. But I will not leave it for Willy to read on his return. I will burn it, for there is no good that can come of it. He will never know.

What can I do to save George? Oh, if only I had the freedom to go to him! Or at least write! But I am a prisoner, a rich little girl surrounded by gaolers. If only I had a real friend!

Fitzwilliam Darcy

Rosings, March 24

We went to the parsonage today.

I had steeled myself to avoid betraying any sign of emotion upon seeing Eliza again. I believe I succeeded, outwardly. It was difficult, however, for me to carry on an acceptable level of conversation for the first few minutes. Her rosy complexion and dark bewitching eyes still held their sway upon my soul, as much as, or perhaps even more than before. No, my mind did not embark on delusional false memories all winter… She is as beautiful as I remember. I had to remain very quiet after our first exchanges. I fear that I appeared again somewhat boorish.

James, naturally, compensated for my stupidity. They conversed a while. I was able, at least, to say a few words to her friend Miss Lucas. Rather, Mrs. Collins. How pitiable is that poor woman's lot. It almost nauseates me to think that Eliza might have accepted Mr. Collins and be lost to me forever.

Finally, I walked over to the Colonel and Eliza, and we engaged in some less than satisfactory conversation; I don't know why it is so difficult for me to be more like James, or Bingley. No problem at all for them to rattle on about this and that with the ladies. At one point, I was rather alarmed. Eliza informed me that her sister Jane had been in town these three months, and she asked me with a curious air whether I had never seen her there. For a moment I feared that she and her sister had seen me at the theater that night—before I ran away like a fool. But I recovered myself instantly and answered with aplomb that I had not. It is a lie, of course. I am not happy with myself for being untruthful. But I had no choice.

In any case, it is clear that my inclination for Miss Eliza is not mere schoolboy silliness, for James, who is no gadfly or knave, was quite taken with her. On our way back to Rosings, he was full of praise for her. "A woman of substance…uncommonly well-spoken…full of wit…and damn good-looking." He was also full of questions to me about her. I evaded them all stolidly. I also detected a dark feeling in my breast toward James…if I am honest, I must call it by its name: jealousy. He conversed so easily with her. She smiled at him, lovely, genuine smiles.

This is unconscionable. What is the matter with me? James is my best friend!

He talked of returning there tomorrow. Well, let him go. Let them prattle away. I do not think I should go again so soon. In fact, I should not see her again until I have quite made up my mind. This is a sort of torture—but what choice do I have?

I wish I had brought Gulliver with me.

Georgiana

London, March 26

Today I was caught in a moment of weakness, but with such happy consequences!

Mr. Hudson had just left after our music lesson, and Mrs. Annesley had gone to her chamber to rest (her wicked migraines!). I was alone, listlessly practicing, feeling all the weight of the burden of knowing George was unhappy and about to marry without love —Miss King—whoever she may be—it all overwhelmed me. I dissolved in a flood of tears. What I did not know was that, having forgotten some sheets of music, Mr. Hudson had quickly returned to the music room. He found me in tears. He is so kind. He feared that he had done something to upset me. When I protested that he was not at all to blame, he still looked so concerned. He said I could confide in him, that he would never betray me. That he understood that I felt quite alone and that he wanted to be seen as a friend.

I had a sudden inspiration. Perhaps Mr. Hudson was sent to me by Providence! He might be my go-between. He could at least deliver a message to be posted and sent to George! So I told him I was very grieved by the possible loss of my second cousin (yes, I lied—but not by much, really) who was in the militia. I was weeping, I said, because I had no way to send him my love and best wishes. Mr. Hudson looked alarmed. I assured him not to think the worst of this. That it was not a romantic sort of *billet doux*…just a note so that he would know he was not so alone in the world, that I was thinking of him in his moment of peril, as he was due to perhaps be shipped off to some dreary place of combat.

He pledged that he would send the note.

So tonight, I am writing to George.

My friend, dare I call you my Brother?

I have found a trusted courier so that we may again correspond. I have been mad with worry about you! I understand you are to be wed. I hope there is affection on both sides, but I am gripped by the fear that you are entering matrimony for the sake of improving your financial fortunes. If that is so, and you are not quite as much in love as you should be, I beg you to reconsider.

This may sound strange, coming from someone so much younger than you, but I hope you will honor my feelings with just a bit of consideration.

Do not despair. If you are hounded by debts, there are solutions. I am convinced that I can change Willy's mind. I think I may have a witness who may be brought to confess to my brother what happened, so long ago, but it will take time. Have faith and be patient. For the moment, my Brother is at Lady Catherine's, and he informed me that he has planned to stay there quite through to the end of the spring, a singular thing, as he usually does not stay there over a se'ennight. So, we must be patient and await his return. This summer, if you can obtain leave from the regiment, perhaps I can plot a meeting. My brother promised to take me to the sea this summer. Perhaps, when I am more certain of his plans, you can make your way to the spot he will have chosen. Perhaps it will be Brighton. I will have prepared the way, and I will bring you into his presence. With me there, he will not dare harm you. Do you know he is starting to treat me a little more like a grownup woman? He has asked me if I was interested in marrying. And he asked ME for my opinion on the kind of woman HE should marry. Clearly there is reason for hope.

I do hope I get a response.

Fitzwilliam Darcy

Rosings, March 29

It has taken my utmost discipline not to accompany James to the Parsonage at all this week. Every day, he comes back whistling or humming softly, and in my ignorance of what has transpired at the Parsonage, my devilish jealousy is kindled. My imagination goes wild. I have to lecture myself quite sternly.

Whatever this regard, affection, or infatuation of mine is, I know this much: I cannot disregard it. I cannot ignore it. It rules my soul.

At least I know James and Miss Eliza will never be left alone at Mr. Collins's Most Humble Abode, and I do not suspect any misbehavior on anyone's part—James is honorable to a fault—that is not what troubles me. No, I am jealous of HIS having the opportunity to converse, banter, walk about in the gardens perhaps, with HER. To look at her.

Tonight, they are all coming to dine. I almost suggested to my Aunt that I might go fetch the whole party. Caught myself just in time. It will not do at all to raise any suspicions. Damnation! I wish Gulliver were here so I would have an excuse to run myself to exhaustion, for my nerves are worn thin with impatience.

March 30

My God, what a fool I have been not to take advantage of the last few days! All this time I could have spent with Miss Eliza, lost!

After last night, I now know that Miss Eliza is, as my heart insisted as soon as I began to know her, a real gem. She was so at ease, so graceful, and yet still witty and just teasing enough, last night. In the pompous, gaudy setting of Lady Catherine's palace, she was the most beautiful and authentic object. At one point, she went over to Anne and engaged her on I know not what topic, and I will swear that this is the first time I have seen Anne smile so genuinely. The contrast between the two women made me sad for Anne. She had been dressed—I am sure she would not have chosen this accoutrement—in a complicated gown with gaudy orange and red, with a spray of peacock feathers, and a purplish shawl, all of which looked most peculiar (but which later the Lady of the house commended in an aside to us gentlemen as improving the brilliance of her complexion, upon which that oafish cleric embarked on a disquisition of the girl's perfections—I think James and I rolled our eyes in perfect harmony). Eliza, on the other hand, wore a simple pale muslin frock with a large silk ribbon. The gown was low-cut as is the fashion, which in this particular application I applaud. My eyes strayed far too often in that direction.

My aunt of course badgered Miss Elizabeth Bennet with questions. But Eliza was intrepid and remained unflappably polite, though not without a few subtle pokes at the impertinence of her interrogator (who doubtless was not clever enough to understand them). It was a pleasure to witness. James and I exchanged a few glances, perhaps an ill-concealed smirk or two.

I am not upset with Aunt Catherine for being so obnoxious, and this for entirely selfish reasons. The advantage of having a boorish person digging for information is that one may have a great opportunity of garnering facts that a more discreet person would forever be ignorant of.

Thus, I learned after extensive cross-examination that although the five sisters never had a governess (shocking!), Mr. Bennet brought in tutors for French, Latin (but not Greek), Poetry, History, Geography, solfeggio, music, and dancing. Apparently the two younger sisters would have none of it except the dancing, but the elder three took advantage of the lessons.

The impertinent Lady de Bourgh spared no commentary after every good-humored answer that Miss Eliza made. Nothing seems to be beneath her notice, and I would not have been surprised if she had inquired after the number of chamber pots at Longbourn and the frequency of their voiding.

It became obvious to me that the discussion that James and I had with Georgiana held the kernel of truth that is now most important to me: it matters not what our family is like. An individual should not be blamed for the imperfections of family relations.

I would be perfectly angry if anyone insinuated, for example, that our blood connection means that I and my Aunt have similar dispositions or turns of mind. I would be confounded if a young lady that I courted told me that because my aunt is hideously ill-bred, she must refuse my offer. This is a new era. We are free agents, and reason, not servile habits or familiar traditions, should guide our every move.

Therefore, it has been unconscionably unjust of me to assume that because Eliza has horrid connections, she herself is to be rejected. In fact, it augments her merit a thousandfold to have risen above the mediocrity that surrounds her. I must include her sister Jane in this analysis; and now I am more than ever questioning the righteousness of my interference with Bingley. When I return to town, perhaps I shall broach the topic with him again. I feel I should make amends.

But to get back to Miss Eliza. After talking with Anne for a little while, she was approached by James apparently to take up a conversation they had left unfinished the day before; they conversed with energy and spirit. He has been able to forge bonds of trust with her; I could tell from her easy demeanor. I wished to be part of the conversation, but my Aunt monopolized my attention, brought Anne to my side, and proceeded to torture the poor girl (and myself, as a consequence) with her usual tact and discretion.

"Anne, my dear, tell your cousin about that lovely screen you are netting."

"Anne, why not ask your cousin about that chapter in Fordyce's Sermons to Young Women that you found so strange."

Anne answered by monosyllables, and I was getting tired of this tedious conversation.

Finally, my aunt found that the Colonel and the pretty lady were just enjoying themselves too much in their discussion of music and cut short their exchange with a loud self-congratulation on her own lack of talent in that domain. The Colonel promptly asked Miss Eliza to play and sing. He had never been privileged to hear her, as there is no instrument in the parsonage. I was curious to see his reaction. But my aunt, in her rude manner, continued her stentorian declarations into my ear and prevented my enjoyment of the performance, so I took the first opportunity to quit the loudmouth's side and I joined James by the pianoforte.

Regrettably, Eliza interrupted her playing when I approached, and she and James started teasing me about my allegedly dreadful demeanor in Hertfordshire. I was happy just to be in her vicinity and far from the ogress, so I smiled good-humoredly.

However, it did look like she still harbored some resentment against me as she faulted me for acting very ill-bred in Hertfordshire. As our last earnest conversation dated back to that accursed ball at Netherfield, I was wondering whether she was still angry with me for my cruel treatment of Wickham. Again, I lost some measure of composure and found it difficult to explain myself. She said not a word about Wickham, however. I suppose she knows he is to be married to an heiress of sorts and therefore is no longer suffering the throes of my neglect and persecution. Ah, if she only knew what designs Wickham had had on my sister! But that is something I cannot ever discuss with her. Suffice it to say that she seems not to be heartbroken at all. I can therefore state with some certainty that she never felt any strong attraction toward Wickham.

Lady Catherine interrupted our conversation, and I was obliged to return to her side. But at least her remarks were fewer, and she eventually dozed off in her great armchair, to everyone's plain relief.

I could see that James found Elizabeth's playing and singing enchanting.

So, it was not just *my* senses being deceived because of a physical attraction. All men of taste would find her damned desirable. Far from an embarrassment, she would make me proud in society. I care not a jot for high society gossip; and if anyone dares reject her when she is mine, they will find themselves rejected by me. At Pemberley, we shall invite those we like.

March 30, Early Morning

Good Lord. I did write those words, last night: "when she is mine."

My admiration and regard for her are quite hopeless.

It seems my soul has taken over my mind. It is time to secure her. I shall go, alone, to the Parsonage, invite her and Miss Lucas—I mean, Mrs. Collins— to walk about, as it is a very fine day, and the birds have been chattering since dawn. I will contrive to have some time alone with her.

March 30, Evening

To my surprise, I found Miss Eliza alone in the Parsonage, as the Collinses had gone on errands in the village. It was quite impossible to ask her to go walking under those conditions. I had to take this opportunity to undertake testing the lady's disposition (Georgiana is quite right about how to deal with undesirable mothers), but I was not quite sure how to go about it, how to introduce the topic of how she would feel if she had to live far away from home. After beating about the bush a while, I became impatient to know her feelings, and sitting closer to her than before, asked her point blank if it were not true that given her disposition, she could not possibly always want to live in Longbourn. I am afraid my manner was too frank, too abrupt. She looked confused, perhaps even alarmed.

I realized my mistake immediately.

I am such a fool. I am like that character in "*She Stoops to Conquer*," who can easily converse with anyone except a woman of true quality. That aspect of my personality brings me no end of misery.

I had to backtrack. Rising from my chair, I switched topics immediately, and my mortification was happily ended by the arrival of Mrs. Collins and her sister.

I must go much more slowly. I must woo her gently. I must find her out of doors. Only in the bosom of nature do our true characters speak out.

March 31, Morning

Earlier today, James and I walked about the lanes for a bit. I was frank with him: I told him that Miss Eliza had undeniable attractions for me, and I wanted there to be no misunderstanding.

He smiled. "I thought that might be the case, Darcy." He laughed. Then, in a theatrical whisper, he said, "I saw her *running*, quite alone in a lane, last week."

I think my jaw dropped open.

"Worry not, Darcy. I would not be your rival, if that's what you are hinting at." He sighed bitterly. "You are a luckier man than me. I must marry a person with a little bit more fortune than 50 pounds at 4%, as our Aunt has helpfully mentioned is all Miss Elizabeth's lot is to be. Lord knows Lady de Bourgh is quick to inform herself of such things."

"She can be useful in a number of ways, including this opportunity for me to become better acquainted with Miss Lizzy."

"Your choice is excellent. I cannot fault your taste, for once. I was nearly sick when I heard you were courting Miss Edwards."

"Actually, so was I. And I am gratified that you condescend to approve of my current choice," I said with a smile.

I let him understand that I would be happy to go with him to the Parsonage every day, but that I would attempt to meet Miss Lizzie every day in the park, just the two of us alone, and would he kindly give me free rein. He graciously agreed, and even promised to eventually let her know that he did not have the power to make an offer to her, in case she had fallen madly in love with him.

We laughed at that.

April 4

These have been the happiest days. I have discovered Lizzie's favorite haunts in the park, and I contrive to meet her accidentally. I think she has understood my machinations and is not displeased. I am much more able to carry on a conversation with her out in the woods, especially when it is just the two of us, than in the confines of parlors and drawing rooms. James is enjoying himself thoroughly, seeing me rather quiet and subdued when we are in company, either at Rosings or at the parsonage, now that he knows my secret. He calls me oafish and stupid out loud for sitting there like a stump, and then winks at me. Fool, but lovable fool! I am glad I was open with him about my feelings. I feel more certain in my designs.

In any case, after these several days and many hours passed with her, given her unfailingly playful disposition, I am convinced I will not have an unhappy moment for the rest of my life, as long as she is with me. We have spoken of anything and everything. She pokes fun at some of my ideas and principles, and to my surprise, it does not bother me. In fact, I am starting to understand some of her points of view, and recasting my own as perhaps too old-fashioned, too "medieval," as she says.

I throw out a few hints now and then of our future stays as a couple in Rosings. She has not really responded to them. Perhaps she is too well-bred to let me know that she understands my meaning completely. But there is no dispute… I am encouraged.

I do long for mornings where I will wake up by her side. Dear God. I am eight-and-twenty and only now do I realize how damned lonely I've been.

April 7

The problem now lies not in whether to propose marriage to Miss Elizabeth, but in how. She knows my affection, I think, but she may believe that I am merely enjoying her company. Given the great disparity between our families' standing, she may (quite rightly) believe that no offer can possibly be made, unless I've lost my mind. And she certainly does not want to marry a dimwit! Therefore, I must be sure to assuage the objections that her reason might put forth.

I must not act like a lovesick knave and make grand passionate declarations. She is beyond doubt one of the most rational women I have ever met. No simpering, no screeching, no whining, no giggling. She will suspect me of playacting if I behave too ardently (although indeed I have dreamed of such theatricals). But it is not in my character to play the stooge, and so, circumspection must be the order of the day.

After mulling this over, I think the best course is for me to lay out in a reasonable manner all the possible perceived impediments first; but then, I shall surprise her by rejecting them all categorically and invoking the strength of my attachment as an unconquerable force. She will be pleased, I think.

Georgiana

London, April 8

When it rains, it pours! I have received two letters today! One came this morning, by way of Mr. Hudson, my faithful courier, and of course was from George. Throughout our lesson, I was so impatient to read it that my fingers tripped over every note. Mr. Hudson was bewildered, and poor Mr. Haydn would have been shocked. But then, when I was finally at leisure to read the letter, what a disappointment! George merely said he had received my note and thanked me for my concern. His duties left him no time to respond to it fully, he would write again by and by, he said. So here I am left wondering what his situation is. Perhaps he does love this Miss King and was offended by my insinuations. I can't do anything properly, it seems. It left me despondent.

But later in the day, I received Willy's letter. It was very different from George's by its length, but also rather mysterious! He writes that when he comes back in May, he will have a wonderful surprise for me. His tone is very different from the usual: he talks of spring leaves budding at Rosings, sunsets, birds chattering, and how he looks forward to seeing me and bringing the surprise. He talks of going to Pemberley later, how he misses me and Gulliver. This is by far the most singular letter he has ever written, with many exclamation points and underscoring, some incoherence, and no questions or advice on my daily activities. I wish he had let me go to Rosings too, as Aunt Catherine had requested. How strange and imperious he can be sometimes! But in this letter, he sounds happy as a lark. Well, I am happy too, then.

Fitzwilliam Darcy

April 9, Early Evening

I can't believe what happened.

She refused me. She *refused* ME!

Because of Wickham! Because of Bingley and Jane Bennet! And, apparently, because she despises me.

All this time, as we ambled down the lanes of Rosings, as we conversed so easily, as I was dreaming of our future bliss, as I foolishly believed her to be delighted by my assiduity, she was secretly detesting me. I have never been so shocked in my life. She called me arrogant and selfish. Ungentlemanly. Said she would never marry me if I was the last man on earth.

All hope is lost.

I have invoked illness and am staying in my chamber. I have dismissed Carruthers for the rest of the day.

April 10, Before Sunrise

I drank two bottles of wine last night, was awfully sick—reached the basin just in time—and finally passed out before midnight. I have just awoken in the dark, as the church bells rang three, and there is a miserable pain in my head and belly.

I feel wretched and exhausted. But I had to light my candles, sharpen more nibs, and sit at the desk, though it cost me a deal of pain. I must do what I must do. I have to write to her. Tell her all the truth. By God, she WILL read it. She has to know who I really am and what Wickham did. I shall hand-deliver the letter to ensure it does not go astray. And then I shall leave her, leave this place immediately, and never see her again.

London, April 12

We came back up to town yesterday.

On the way, James let me know by looks and frowns and muttered questions (which I ignored) that he expected an explanation from me for my strange ill-humor. As the coach rumbled on and the atmosphere was getting thicker, I plunged forth.

"Well, Colonel Fitzwilliam, I did it. I proposed to Miss Elizabeth Bennet."

James's eyes widened, and he stared at me with unabashed amazement. I sat mute. Not by stubbornness, but in truth because I really did not know how to proceed from there. How much or how little to say.

"Darcy, quit staring out the window! Is that all you have to say? Well, have you decided on a date? I wasn't sure you would go through with it, but you did! You are one lucky fellow!"

I was surprised at his enthusiasm. Didn't my dark demeanor indicate that I was far from lucky?

"She refused me."

His jaw dropped open and he gaped at me.

"She refused you? But—"

"Do you mind if we don't speak of this? I am in no humor to rehearse this miserable episode. I thank you for your adherence to my wishes for you to NOT think of this lady for your own purposes when I detected an inclination on your part. You are hereby relieved of any obeisance to my injunctions in that regard."

"Darcy, you insult me. Stop this nonsensical behavior and please tell me what happened—at least, the reason for her refusal."

I remained silent. He cursed under his breath.

"Well, do what you like. Wallow in your misery. But know that I will lend an ear and will keep your secrets faithfully. As for my inclination, I did find Miss Eliza as charming as possible, but I know she is beyond my reach in several respects."

I smiled, perhaps bitterly, but said nothing. Presently he sighed, closed his eyes, leaned back, and was soon fast asleep. No such release was afforded to my burdened mind. Her angry eyes haunted me, her accusations kept ringing in my ears.

About an hour later, James was roused by a particularly violent jolting of the coach. I could not tolerate the drumming of my reflections anymore, and in the depths of misery, anger, and humiliation, took his advice.

"She refused me on three counts," I said as soon as he was done yawning and stretching his limbs.

"Three. My God, Darcy! Wouldn't just ONE have amply sufficed?"

"Indeed. I received a veritable catalogue of excellent reasons why she thought I was the last man on earth she could ever be prevailed on to marry. That is a direct quote from the lady."

"Well. I understand now your rotten mood and your impatience to leave Rosings."

"The first volley had to do with—but perhaps you remember what I related to you on our way to Rosings? About a friend whom I vehemently advised not to enter into an engagement with a girl of dubious relations? Well, that friend is Bingley, and the girl was Miss Eliza's beloved sister Jane. God knows how she found out my role in this."

James turned a deep shade of purple.

"Oh hell. Oh hell. Oh hell. Me and my big mouth," he muttered.

"What the devil do you mean?"

"Darcy, I beg you not to crush my face. I am the culprit."

"What?"

"On one of my strolls with Miss Eliza, ah…just a few days ago… I mentioned your triumph in just such a situation."

My anger, already at a simmering point, exploded. "Damn it, James! Whatever possessed you? How dare you discuss my private affairs?"

Well, there is no need for me to rehearse the insults and profanity that spewed forth from my mouth. To his credit, Fitzy looked supremely uncomfortable. He produced a flask and offered it to me. I grabbed it and emptied it in one long draught. That felt good. And it loosened my tongue. Though I resumed accusing and berating him, he did not seem to mind that much. He would just nod and smile sheepishly. Finally, when I found I was repeating myself excessively, I clamped my mouth shut.

"So, that was the first. What were the other two objections? I hope they weren't my fault as well?" he asked. He smiled broadly, but he was not mocking me. His eyes were kind.

James has an amiable disposition. The thought crossed my mind that he was better suited than I was for Elizabeth. But I didn't like that thought and dismissed it, even though, at this point, what did it matter?

"Perhaps you know she had a fairly intimate acquaintance with George Wickham while he was quartered at Meryton. The miscreant apparently told her that I turned him out penniless upon my father's passing. She was quite indignant at my cruelty toward him."

"But those are lies! It is well known that he refused the living and took a handsome sum instead! Darcy, once she is apprised of the facts, she will no longer hold this against you. But—perhaps you can't tell her…all the facts…on account of Georgiana…"

"Worry not. I related the entire history of Mr. Wickham and his attempt on my sister in a letter that I remitted to her on the eve of our departure."

"Ah, well then. I do think she is rational. She will believe you."

"I gave her leave to apply to you for verification of the entire history."

"I shall be happy to do it forthwith in a letter if you like!"

"You forget there is a third objection."

"Ah yes."

"Number three, I am afraid, has no remedy: she hates me."

When James countered that this last point seemed implausible, as her demeanor had indicated no such implacable resentment, I explained that her manners prevented such visible abuse toward me, but I did relate the epithets hurled at me: arrogant, conceited, ungentlemanlike. The last seemed to surprise him.

"Were you ever ungentlemanlike?" James asked.

I sensed a prickling of my conscience. I had rehearsed my proposal many times since the rejection. I was quiet, but James would not let that question go unanswered. At length, I said that the manner of my proposal may not have been the most felicitous. And upon more prodding, I related the little speech I had made listing the objections I had had to surmount.

Fitzy was unable to repress the urge, and he exploded into laughter. I looked at him darkly.

"Darcy. Forgive me. But you must see that she merely gave you your due for such insults! Are you daft? What man in his right mind ever proposed in that way?"

"I am sorry. I lack practice in that too, I suppose," I said bitterly.

"You were a complete fool."

"Thank you for that." I was miffed. I did not like James's continued ill-concealed hilarity. I told him I had given him the information he desired, and would he do me the honor of never referring to this subject again. I pretended to slumber the rest of the way.

Georgiana

London, April 14, Early Morning

Fitzy and Willy arrived last night. I was quite shocked, not just by their premature and unannounced return, but by my brother's brusque and diffident manner, as if something quite dreadful had happened. He mumbled a greeting of sorts, hardly even looked at me, did not bother to sit, but hurried off to his chamber. Even worse, Fitzy looked depressed, nary a smile, nothing but grave looks and a set jaw. When I begged him to tell me what was the matter, he whispered to me not to inquire, that he would explain later.

Today, my brother left the house before I was even dressed. No sign of Fitzy either. I can't fathom what happened. It seems the great surprise Willy had promised me is not for now. What is wrong with these men?

April 14, Late at Night

Perhaps it was wrong of me to engage in snooping among my brother's things. But when the opportunity arose for me to enter his chamber today while he was out, I could not resist. On his desk were various papers, but one of them I found quite interesting: another letter from the spy. As it had been unsealed and presumably read, I picked it up with no qualms.

It said that "Wickham and his betrothed have broken off their engagement, quite suddenly. No reason has been put forth, but it is easy to guess that she realized she can do better than this rogue, despite her less-than-attractive looks, for a good fortune has a magical way of enticing penniless young men, and there are plenty of those to go around. In other news, one of the Bennet sisters is very intimate with Colonel Forster's young wife," etc., etc. He related more village gossip and said that the regiment is rumored to leave Meryton soon and be encamped at Brighton for the summer.

The important thing is that George, from this account, must have taken my advice seriously after all! I would wager that he is the one who broke off the engagement. He is so handsome and well-spoken, and from Captain Pratt's account, it seems Miss King must be very plain indeed. I do not believe *she* would want to let him go. I am a little worried because this spy is calling George a rogue! It can't be true. In any case, I am so happy he listened to me and decided not to marry Miss King. I am sure to receive a letter from him soon, explaining all that happened.

April 30

I still do not know what happened at Rosings to make my brother and cousin quit the place so abruptly and return in such ill humor. They have been back two weeks already, and I have not been able to get anything out of either of them. I find it very odd that Fitzy especially has kept such a guarded silence. I know I am a great favorite of his, and this treatment leaves me sad and lonely.

Sometimes I hear them arguing—well, not really arguing, but discussing things very earnestly when they are alone together, but as soon as I creep forward, they hear me and their tone changes completely.

What on earth happened at Rosings? Did my brother have a quarrel with Aunt Catherine or my cousin Anne? I wonder if my aunt's character worsened to the point that she threatened Willy with some sort of retribution if he did not propose to Anne forthwith. That might explain things. My poor brother has told me that Lady Catherine imagines that our mother's dying wish was to see this union go forth. Poor Anne! Though she loves Willy well enough, it's a brotherly love, she told me, and she says she never wants to wed. I wrote her a very general letter (but still with a few questions that I hope she might answer), but I haven't received her reply yet.

May 1

Strangely enough, I received a letter from Anne this morning! To my question of how she had enjoyed having visitors and what her occupations were this spring, she answered with the usual generalities. This was to be expected. I know Aunt Catherine reads all incoming and outgoing correspondence (poor Anne!).

But there was something extremely interesting in that letter, which is setting my mind a-fluttering. She said she was, as usual, very sad at the departure of her cousins but also, a little bit later, at that of the parson's visitors, Sir William Lucas and his daughter Maria, as well as Mrs. Collins's friend, Miss Elizabeth Bennet, who she said was very kind and very obliging, playing the pianoforte and singing whenever it was requested. I noticed that her handwriting took a slightly different slant in the following sentence: *"Miss Bennet has been very kind with me, entertaining me with descriptions of a play in London that she enjoyed very much; but some aspects of her demeanor I am sure I will not emulate, such as running in the lanes, all alone. "*

Running? I wonder…might Miss Bennet be at the heart of this mystery?

PART III

Fitzwilliam Darcy

London, May 15

The despondency and melancholy humor that used to plague my mother seem to be part and parcel of my existence now. Perhaps it is a familial disease. It had lifted soon after I made the acquaintance of the Bennet family, first in my infatuation with Jane, and then with my deeper, more serious regard, no, let me write the word, love, for Miss... Oh, I dare not even write her name, for a flood of pain and longing overcomes me when I think of her.

And I think of her every day. I do my best to keep as busy as possible to avoid time for reflection. Bingley seems to need the distractions as much as I do. I understand his dejection, for if he still cares for Miss Bennet as much as I do for her sister, we are indeed fellow sufferers. If I had any real strength of character, I would tell him to damn it all and if he wants his Jane to go and get her. But it would pain me too much, because I would then be completely bereft. No, let his affections simmer down and slowly evaporate, as I wish mine would.

In this regard, Caroline and Louisa are very useful to us, for they have taken it upon themselves to keep us in a flurry of activities. Those women, so languid in most respects, become veritable maestras where social engagements are concerned. Dinners, theatre, music, exhibitions. It never stops! I feel I have been transformed into a mindless fop, a poseur in this merry-go-round of worldly pursuits that lead to naught. But better to be thus consumed than muddle through the swamp of stinging memories.

My ill-fated declaration haunts me, more punishingly every day. I think back on my idiotic rhetoric, in how ugly a light it placed my regard. My entire demeanor makes me cringe now. I rehearse endlessly our last conversation, I see again her flashing black eyes, her heightened color, the set of her chin... And although her discourse angered me greatly, even then, even in the midst of her accusations and contempt, I admired her. As I think back, I admire her still. How well she voiced her objections. Any other female would have shrieked or thrown a vase, or stomped out of the room. But not her.

"Had you behaved in a more gentlemanlike manner…"

"Your mode of declaration merely spared me the concern…"

"Your arrogance, your conceit…"

Had this scene been in the pages of *Udolfo*, as the hero I surely would have taken the beautifully angry damsel in my arms and kissed her. She would have melted into my embrace. All would have been explained and forgiven.

But this was the world of reality, and I, poor excuse for a hero, had to retreat. The best I could do was write that letter. Although I do not recall its contents very clearly, I am constantly tortured by the possibility that it may have contained more of the hideous language which had worked so well for me a few hours before. What has she thought of it? Did she even read it? Did she believe what I told her about Wickham? Did she burn it in anger?

Well, it's time to dress for dinner. Caroline, who has been less zealously by my side than last summer—perhaps my cold manner has definitively discouraged her—has invited a few society matrons and their marriageable daughters. Georgiana is to perform for them tonight and has been practicing all day. At least I can look forward to that.

May 26

This evening, Bingley told me abruptly that it was exactly six months ago today that the ball at Netherfield took place. He had a strange look, more piercing than usual, somewhat questioning. I may have read some accusation in his tone. I had the audacity to ask him in as cold a manner as I could muster, if he still held Miss Bennet in the same regard as he did then.

He confessed he did. "I have found no one among any of our acquaintance here who has the same happy combination of beauty, sense, manners, disposition."

"Miss Bennet was indeed rather unusual," I responded shortly. "But not unique. Didn't you enjoy dancing with Lord Cavendish's daughter last week?"

"I did. But there was nothing more to enjoy. Her head is as empty as a sparrow's. And did you enjoy your supper conversation with Miss Carter, Darcy?" he asked teasingly.

"I must admit I was bored silly."

This is ridiculous. We are like two lovesick puppies, pining after our country damsels. Bingley looked at me earnestly, and I am certain that he wanted to talk further. Like a coward, I ended the conversation there and quitted his company on a flimsy pretext. I feared he would ask questions that would perturb me greatly…for example, should he go back to Netherfield? Had I heard anything of all those officers visiting Longbourn? Was it such a problem that the mother and some of the sisters were so ill-behaved in public? This would lead to his remarking that Elizabeth was also a superior woman…and then I would be quite lost, and this might break my resolve of aloofness.

I think what I did was, again, for the best.

Georgiana

London, May 30

My brother says we are to return to Pemberley in a se'ennight. He is evidently out of humor with town life. He has been out of sorts, acting very strange. In company he used to be alert and conversant and often amused his guests or hosts with pleasing anecdotes. No more of that. He sits morosely. He has been avoiding me. I had started a conversation with him, quite innocently, saying that cousin Anne had talked of visitors from Hertfordshire... He looked alarmed, smiled briefly, and almost ran out of the room. I am nonplussed, but I believe indeed this is where all his misery stems from.

In any case, I was not able to have any private conversation with him. Now he declares that we will be off soon, and when I protested a bit, he promised that we should return in a month or two, but nothing was very definite. Fitzy is leaving tomorrow. I had hoped he could come to Pemberley with us, but that will not be the case.

Unfortunately, at Pemberley there will be no Mr. Hudson to mail and receive letters for me, so my planning and scheming have all gone to naught. Again.

I wish again, for the millionth time, that I were a man, although I would really hate to be a man. Let's say that I wish that as a woman I had the same liberties as a man.

I hate this life of dependency. I am at the mercy of everyone, for everything, all the time.

Gulliver

Pemberley, June 15

Master Willy has been back for a week now, and life is delicious, except for those waves of misery that I can sniff a mile away.

He should not go to town. Every time he comes back, it takes him days to recover.

The first few nights, he was like a madman. Getting up at all hours, drinking, writing things, and throwing the paper in the fire.

I think he is happiest when he is outside with me, as we traverse hills and fields. And do we cover a lot of ground! I get him nice and tired so he will sleep with no troubles. And it's working. Finally, he is sleeping a little better.

He should not mix with all these imbecile humans who act like ants, fighting and working all day. Or like crows, who caw endlessly. And for what, I ask you? I swear I will catch one soon, and it will be pure joy to feel its little bones crack under my teeth. I don't care for their nasty feathers, though.

Miss Georgie is a little odder too since they've returned. I sense some worries and troubles. She isn't a child anymore, alas. Getting taller. I notice these things.

I hope she doesn't become like that mushroom girl. No, there is no chance of that…she still loves me and pets me endlessly.

Georgiana

Pemberley, June 20

I am so frustrated! No news from George, nothing. And Willy has gone back to town this morning. I overheard him telling Mrs. Reynolds he would send for me in a few weeks. No real news from Anne, even though I asked her to tell me a little more about her visitors from Hertfordshire. No Mrs. Prescott visiting. No whispered conversations to eavesdrop on.

I run around in circles in my head. Outwardly, of course, I am a good girl, practicing my music daily. I have embarked on a huge embroidery project, quite a tapestry, featuring ponds and peacocks. I shall turn thirty before I ever finish it, but no matter. Anything to keep my hands and brain busy just a bit.

I am trying to work the mystery out. Miss Elizabeth Bennet is certainly that pretty woman who runs. He met her in Hertfordshire when he was at Netherfield with the Bingleys, that is certain. He met her again at Rosings. Something happened, and he left abruptly, and he has been miserable since. Fitzy was a witness. Or…did Fitzy fancy her? Did they have a falling out over her?

Oh, this is so puzzling. But wait… I have an idea! Perhaps my Aunt would be a willing informant…unwittingly. Since Anne is unable to write her thoughts to me, due to the censorship of her monstrous mother, let me write to the monster herself, and ask *her* very specifically about Miss Elizabeth Bennet.

Pemberley, June 29

I am amazed at my success and at the swiftness of my aunt's response. It did yield some interesting clues.

"Regarding Miss Elizabeth Bennet, yes, my dear niece! I am overjoyed that you ask for my guidance. I did instruct Anne not to imitate that young woman! and I am glad to impart to you the same wisdom, from which well-bred young ladies must learn. Miss Elizabeth Bennet is not without qualities. While your Brother and the Colonel were here, she was very useful in providing

entertainment for them. I believe the gentlemen must have gone to the Parsonage daily, which vexed me, as Anne was being most egregiously neglected. But how does one get through to young men these days?

"Miss Elizabeth Bennet's performance on the pianoforte, I declare, is very inferior to yours, my dear Georgiana, but the gentlemen seemed to enjoy it thoroughly, and were quite vocal in requesting her performance again and again. Her singing is not intolerable. Anne would have been much more of a favorite at the instrument, if her ill health had not prevented her learning. We spent many an evening thus dividing our attention between cards and music.

"But here I must be frank. The Colonel and Miss Elizabeth Bennet also spent a lot of time conversing in private on several occasions while we were all together in the petit salon after supper: this I must point out to you as a sign of grievous ill-breeding. They kept the rest of the company quite bereft, and I had to call James to attention on that account, requesting that they might condescend to include us in their spirited exchanges. Take warning, dear niece, that while elders are present, most of your attention should be due to them.

"Another aspect of her personality was an outspokenness that I have not witnessed in many young ladies her age. Refrain from doing this, Georgiana, and do not encourage it in others, especially of lower standing. No person of rank wants an inferior woman to prattle on and display her opinions on every topic imaginable.

"And lastly, and I had a long talk with her on the eve of her departure on this topic, one must maintain the utmost decorum at all times! I was informed that she had been seen running in the lanes, quite alone, without her bonnet. This cannot be tolerated in a young woman of virtue! and I made her promise most solemnly that she would never again indulge in this kind of wild behavior, here or elsewhere! I am quite sure that you never partake in such low deportment, but…" etc., etc.

Well!!! Thank you, Aunt, for your thorough report! I couldn't help but laugh at these descriptions and exclamatory exhortations. I can imagine the scenes in the *petit salon*, poor Anne sitting in pure misery at her mother's miserable behavior, and poor Miss Elizabeth Bennet having to suffer the slings and arrows of outrageous Lady de Bourgh. I wonder how my cousin and brother behaved during all of this. But of course, they escaped to the Parsonage every day… Well, now I am convinced that the person who is wreaking such havoc in my brother's heart must be Miss Elizabeth Bennet.

I like that name.

I arrived in town yesterday, and this morning I did it! I asked my brother pointblank about Miss Elizabeth Bennet.

We were alone, just the two of us, finishing breakfast. He had dismissed the servants and was telling me that he was going to be out most of the day, apologizing for leaving me alone on my first day back in town. I looked at him steadily and said: "Before you go, please tell me about Miss Elizabeth Bennet."

He turned awfully pale.

"Who told you anything about her?" he asked. "The colonel!" he exclaimed.

"No, brother, not at all. Cousin Anne wrote me about her, and so did Aunt Catherine. They both said she was a frequent visitor at Rosings while you were there. Anne said she was very pretty but that her mother disapproved of her. Aunt wrote that she engaged in reprehensible behavior. I was simply curious as to your opinion of what reprehensible behavior is. I need to know those things." I smiled at him sweetly. I can look very innocent when I want to.

To my surprise, he laughed. "Pray tell me, first, what our cousin and aunt have to accuse her of."

"Oh, Anne was rather vague, merely saying Lady Catherine was oft displeased with Miss Bennet. But my aunt's letter mentioned a horrid frankness…"

"Indeed, Miss Bennet is very honest," he said. I noticed a flash in his eyes and a brief clenching of his jaw, but he recovered quickly and smiled. "Anything else?"

"Let me think." I pretended to search my memory, though I had practically learned the fault-finding letter by heart. I watched his eyes, they were earnestly glued to mine. "Ah yes, she lacks accomplishment and does not play very well."

He made a face. "Untrue. She may not be quite as accomplished in playing the instrument as you are, Georgiana, but the Colonel and I both had great pleasure in listening to her. Her singing is, in my opinion, among the best."

"And she and the Colonel ignored the company and had long conversations in tête-à-tête, which Aunt says was very impolite."

"That only happened a couple of times, and not for very long durations. James is more to blame, as I recall. Miss Bennet's manners are impeccable."

"But the very worst is yet to come. Prepare yourself, brother." I made a dramatic pause and watched his anxious eyes. "My aunt says that she runs. Runs in the park. Often bareheaded. Alone. So here we have a very pretty woman who likes to run." My eyes were fixed on him as I said that, and I saw an amazing, almost frightening change in his countenance. He was certainly recalling our conversation on New Year's Eve. He looked down, put his elbows on the table and his head in his hands. He was quiet a little while.

"Georgiana," he finally said, "you are too clever by far."

"Brother, I am not sure I understand you."

"I think you do. I think you have guessed that I have developed the deepest attachment to Miss Elizabeth Bennet."

"Is *she* the woman with a monstrous mother then?"

"Yes."

"And is that why you have been so despondent since your return from Rosings? On account of the mother?"

"No." He breathed a deep sigh and looked at me. He had a sad smile. "I had made my peace with the mother being a wretch, and was ready to follow your advice, which if you recall was to secure the lady and then stay far away from the mother."

I shook my head. "So why…what happened?"

"Well, Georgiana, since you seem to have grown up quite a bit, I can tell you all, or almost all."

This was a good beginning. I could not believe my luck. I thought to myself that sometimes, the best thing to do is simply ask…and not give up.

He rose and walked about the room a bit. Then, in choppy sentences that are not at all his style, he related meeting the Bennet sisters in Hertfordshire, Bingley falling for the elder, he himself finding the next sister at first unusual, then interesting, then intelligent, beautiful, and charming; but he had qualms about associating with a family that often lacked decorum.

"But you said that her manners were impeccable."

"They are. And her sister Jane's are as well."

"So then it's just the rest of the family." An awful thought came to me. "Oh, you didn't discourage Charles, brother, did you?"

"I confess I did."

"No wonder he has been looking so sad."

"Do you think I acted badly in that regard?"

"Well, he is his own master, I should think. If he really loved Miss Bennet, your opinion should not count for so much."

"Bingley is a humble sort and I was able to convince him that the lady was not as enamored of him as he was of her."

"Were you telling the truth?"

He laughed softly. "Dear sister, you could consider a career in law if you were a man. Was I telling the truth? I hardly know now. I think I wanted it to be the truth."

"But in *your* case, what happened, since you just said you had made your peace with the low connections of the family?"

"In my case, I made an offer of marriage to Miss Elizabeth Bennet, and she refused me."

I was so astonished I think I left my mouth open a good half-minute.

The silence hung quite thick.

"How could she refuse you? You are everything that is amiable and intelligent!"

"Perhaps she didn't see it that way."

"I'm sorry, brother, but…what did she say? What was her reason?"

"She had several, but among them was my arrogant intrusion into her sister's affairs."

"Ah, so the sister DID love Charles!"

"That is what Miss Elizabeth claims."

"Then it must be true. Sisters, I believe, are often in each other's confidence."

He smiled at my rather sad tone. "She was the surprise I had overconfidently promised you. I was convinced you would like her, and she would like you. And you would finally have the sister you have wanted all your life."

"You still have great regard for her despite her rejection."

"I do. I may have acted very foolishly in many respects. I am afraid that unwittingly I was quite insulting toward her family in my proposal. I now think she had good reason to reject me."

"But if you make amends, confess all to Mr. Bingley, and go back to her and ask her forgiveness—I know that is hard to do, but sometimes we have no choice—well, don't you think there is reason for hope?"

"I'm afraid not. I feel someone has poisoned her mind as to my character. She called me arrogant and conceited. She doesn't like me and told me so." He had a short, bitter laugh. "So you see, Aunt Catherine is right, the lady possesses a high level of frankness."

I knew how difficult it was for Willy to talk to me so openly about something so painful and so private. I was afraid he would close up his armor again and the pain would fester. I had to keep some hope alive in him.

"There must have been some misunderstanding. Someone lied about you. I wish I could meet her. Does she ever go to town?"

"Very seldom, from what I gather. And if you think you might want to try your hand at playing Cupid, remove all such thoughts from your mind. I am not keen to receive a second refusal."

There. His voice had sharpened, his stance stiffened. The armor of pride had gone back up. As visitors were now being announced, this ended our conversation.

But now I know almost everything. While I understand that my brother's interference in the sister's love affair was cause for anger on Miss Elizabeth's side—for I am sure there was love on both sides, judging from Charles's demeanor lately—I cannot believe that anyone could find Willy arrogant and conceited to such a degree. I may be biased as a sister, but most people agree that he is exceedingly handsome. And I know he is kind. This seems to have not mattered a bit. Well, one thing is certain. She is not a fortune hunter, and she adheres to principles. I am extremely curious to meet her, but cannot imagine how I could contrive that.

What a shame for Willy—and me—that she said no. If she had said yes, how different all our lives would be right now!

July 9

I had another opportunity to talk privately with Willy. With my novel approach to truth seeking in the direct mode, I asked him to tell me more specifically about Miss Elizabeth. He had a little crooked smile that was half pain, half joy. But he responded!

"What would you like to know?"

"I would like to know what it is about her that has caught your fancy. Tell me what you can, what you will. I will be content with crumbs if I cannot have the entire cake."

He laughed. "All right. She is unique among women of my acquaintance. She is beautiful in an honest, authentic, natural way. She has a winning smile. Her eyes are expressive. Her thinking is flawless, her discourse agile and pertinent. I may have been the target of her wit occasionally, and you know, it was done so playfully that it was enjoyable to me. But she can maintain the highest level of decorum in society."

"How did Anne like her?"

"Very much, I think, though as you know, our cousin is the most reticent person in the world. I watched Anne closely, she would follow Miss Eliza's movements and conversation with assiduity. She seemed to long to be friendlier with her guest, but you know, with our Aunt there…"

"Yes. Difficult indeed."

"I have not met her equal in society in the last eight years. The person she resembles the most in seriousness, good humor, and resolve might be you, Georgiana."

"Indeed, I must consider myself flattered."

"But this flattery is truthful. She is older than you, of course, so she has had a few more years to sharpen her skills in society."

"Brother, she sounds like a person I would really want to meet! Please, do you think you could make it happen?"

"No."

He sounded sure of his fact.

I told him he was too morose. I lectured him (my, how we have switched roles in the last year!). I told him he had to do his best, and hope for the best, and he would be surprised how time and the secret clockwork of the universe would conspire to help his pursuits.

"Many a time I have come across a piece of music that was impossible at first. My fingers would stumble and I could not apply the tempo. I would have given up. But Mr. Hudson would smile and say, let it sit, let it simmer overnight. Don't think of it. Practice, then forget it. Practice again, then forget it. It will work itself out."

"And…?"

"And inevitably it did. My fingers would do what they needed to do without my dogged interference."

"And you think there would be identical results when it comes to human relations? When a person, by her own admission, is so determinedly set against me, miraculously the resentment would melt away, by my practicing? Practicing at what—believing it would? You really think it would work?"

"I don't merely think so, Willy. I guarantee it." I smiled at him. I was not at all certain of my facts, my theory lacked any sort of support or proof, but I had to project a strong demeanor in the face of his stubbornness.

First, he smiled, and then he laughed outright, the good laugh from his earlier years. "Ah, Georgiana, you little fey!" he said before we parted.

Oh well, I cannot assume all will miraculously turn out for the best. But I must believe it will.

Fitzwilliam Darcy

London, July 11

Back in town, I find the heat and the dust almost unbearable. I already miss Gulliver and the cool dales of Pemberley. But I feel better. The long rambles I took through the summer woods with Gulliver and the better understanding and confidence I now have with Georgiana have helped clear my head and soothe my heart a bit. When Georgiana exhibited such sorrow and surprise at my having been refused, for some reason some of that burden was taken off my soul. Of course, I could not explain that George Wickham also played a role in Miss Elizabeth Bennet's refusal.

I did wrong by Bingley and Miss Bennet. I was callous and cowardly. On that count, Elizabeth was right. I cannot fault her for being angry. Georgiana says I must make amends. Perhaps I shall. But Bingley and his sisters are in Bath for the next three weeks. I could join them there, but I would prefer to make my confession to Charles at Pemberley. Somehow, things are clearer and more authentic in the setting that I love above all else.

Perhaps I shall invite Charles (and the inevitable appendages, Caroline and the Hursts) to Pemberley in August. In the shaded lanes, I shall find an opportunity to have a talk with Charles. I shall tell him that I have reason to believe that Miss Bennet does have strong feelings for him, that she is not being courted by anyone, and that if he still feels the way he did, he might as well find out for himself.

I almost hope he jumps on a horse and rides all the way to Longbourn, for my conscience has been needling me most acutely lately. Georgiana's look when she asked if I had meddled was piercing and painful. As if she was finding out for the first time that her most perfect brother could sometimes be in the wrong. Clearly, my thinking has been egregious, my behavior ugly.

In short, I've been an ass.

I must make reparations. In fact, as I write these words, I find I am impatient to do so.

As for Miss Elizabeth Bennet, I am afraid my sister is wrong and that nothing can bring us together now. I still wonder whether she believed anything in my letter. Or even read it. Maybe, if she was as angry as I was when I received George's letter, maybe she burned my letter like I burned his.

Georgiana Darcy

London, July 30

I am so impatient to go back to Pemberley! But we still have to wait a week or so, until my brother has finished with some business here. Nothing is of interest here to me, now that Mr. Hudson left. He has been gone almost a week now. I was wretched when he explained he was going to North America to seek his fortune there. I think I had developed affection for him. I think about him every day. When we finished our last lesson, he looked at me sadly and muttered goodbye, saying what an honor it had been for him to have me as a student. I think if things were different here in England, he might have said more to me. I did not know what to say, but I hugged him when Mrs. Annesley was not looking.

I shall probably never see him again, for it's very unlikely that I shall be running off for those frozen lands of beavers and bears! In these warring times, I do hope he makes the crossing safely.

One other awful consequence of his departure, of course, is that I have no more messenger. But it does not signify much, since George has not written to me in ages. I have decided not to think about George until he makes an effort to communicate with me. I am a bit cross with him.

August 3

Finally! our day of departure draws near. Willy left yesterday ahead of us on horseback, and I shall be riding in the carriage with the Hursts and Caroline Bingley tomorrow. I do not look forward to it. But as they were all in Hertfordshire together, I might make use of my newfound ability to extract information by asking well-thought-out questions. Perhaps the long hours closeted with those three will go by a bit more swiftly.

I hope Mr. Hurst does not snore the entire way, and I pray he bathes before we leave.

Gulliver

Pemberley, August 4, Afternoon

A most excellent day! First, Master Willy is back. He arrived all sweaty and dusty, took his horse to the stable himself, and I am sure he was eager to go refresh himself, but he took some time to be with me. I gave him a nice, noisy welcome. He laughed like he used to when I was a puppy, a full-throated laugh, so happy to see me. Well, who wouldn't be? In fact, there was a surprise! That very nice girl, Miss Lizzie, came here too, and she was excited to see me too. I didn't think I would see her again, but it seems she travels as much as Master Willy.

Anyway, there I was, taking Master Willy for his walk after he had eaten and changed his clothes, when I came upon her scent. She was in the other lane and hidden from sight. I know humans can't detect people unless they perceive them with their eyes, which I pity them greatly for. But you better believe I have not forgotten her, and though she was far away I knew exactly who she was and where she was. So, I ran in her direction, barking a bit, unheeding of my master's commands. I outran him, of course, and there she was by the pond, and she gave me those nice scratches, she has the perfect touch, good fingernails. Then a few minutes later, he arrived upon us at a corner of the lane. He appeared from behind a hedge, all panting and puffing. And what a great to-do that was! Humans would not see it, of course, but I sensed it. Both of them. All aquiver and fluttering. So strange, but I had sensed something like that before, last year, in Hertfordshire.

She could hardly breathe. Then she said Mr. Darcy! He said Miss Bennet! And then they both mumbled. Incoherent at first, and then it all seemed to calm down. She smiled. I sensed something new from her. Something good and strong and soft at the same time. I am not sure Master Willy perceived it though.

Poor humans, what they miss with their wretched lack of abilities…

So I tried to help. Oh, I let them know, him and her, what was what. Bouncing, running from one to the other. Short barks. Puppy dog looks, whines. Tail flapping. But all my efforts were in vain. I'm back in the stables, and I suppose it would not kill me to take a good nap, after all my exertions.

Fitzwilliam Darcy

Pemberley, August 4, Nearing Midnight

She came. She came to Pemberley!

I was strolling about in the woods with Gulliver, when all of a sudden that disobedient animal started barking madly, and he took off, running insanely through the thickets. I followed as well as I could in the paths, and as I turned into the lane, there she was, petting the crazed canine, who seemed to have found a long-lost friend.

I was so shocked I was hardly able to maintain any coherence when I was first able to speak. To be honest, she looked a bit flustered too. A huge wave of emotion washed over me. She looked so beautiful I could have gotten on my knees then and there and begged her forgiveness. Her cheeks were flushed, her eyes…yes, her fine eyes…so bright. As it was quite a warm day, she wore a very becoming muslin gown, low-cut as is the fashion, that enhanced her charms and provoked, once again, that special effect she has on me. Damnation. Hard to maintain decorum sometimes.

I finally was able to enunciate the necessary civilities and understood from her rather unusual babbling that she and others in her party were touring the country and visiting great houses.

"We were on our way to the lakes, but we couldn't because of ah… Mr. Gardiner's business, but Mrs. Gardiner used to live in Derbyshire and so we went to the Peak…and Dove-Dale, and she said Pemberley…was among the finest—" she stopped abruptly and looked at me with something like alarm.

I encouraged her with a smile, which I hope did not appear arrogant or selfish.

"We had inquired ahead of time. I assure you that…we were assured that you…the housekeeper assured us…that the family was…you were…in town…until tomorrow…"

"Indeed, the housekeeper had been told as much. But I was impatient to come home and rode ahead of schedule."

"I am extremely sorry. We should not have come. I must rejoin my friends. We must go."

She was biting her lip. Her flustered manner and her disjointed speech were miles away from her last exchange with me. How well she had remained mistress of her discourse and demeanor then, and what a change now. I was surprised, but for some reason her incoherence made me regain a bit of confidence.

"Please do not apologize. Are those your friends, over in the next lane?"

She assented with a nod.

I could not think of anything to say.

She glanced up at me briefly, curtseyed, and before I could stop her, she hurried away down the lane.

Gulliver started yelping and barking, practically jumped on me, and like a rabid dog, went racing to and fro, from her to me, back and forth. Finally, I was able to restrain him.

"Enough, Gully. Hush!" I took him to the stables and gave orders not to let him out. He was entirely too agitated and excited, as if he was mimicking the turmoil of my mind.

I could not let this opportunity pass. Could this be the occasion that Georgiana had predicted? That little sister of mine has supernatural powers. I understood this was my one chance, that the powers of the universe were granting me my wish, and I had to honor it. I had to strike the iron while it was hot.

I put a bit of order in my attire, as Gulliver had left big dusty pawprints on my waistcoat, and running after the beast had loosened my kerchief. Seeing where the three visitors were headed, I decided to join them by going around the copse in the other direction.

She was walking ahead of the others, a couple who were proceeding rather slowly. As soon as she saw me, she started, but soon rallied, and then calmly proceeded toward me and began to exclaim on the beauties of the park, the delightful views and stately trees. And then she turned very pink and said nothing more. She looked mortified, and I felt sorry for her in her acute embarrassment.

"Pray would you do me the honor of introducing me to your companions?" I asked.

She smiled. "Of course."

We walked toward the fashionable-looking couple. I recognized the woman who had been with Eliza and Jane at the theater. She is Mrs. Gardiner. Her husband, Mr. Gardiner, who is Mrs. Bennet's brother, is about as different from his sister as that youngest Bennet sister is from Jane. Which proves that there can be immense variation among siblings. This whole notion of breeding in favor of which Aunt Catherine is so prepossessed loses much of its validity in my eyes now.

We had a pleasant exchange and walked for a bit along the lake. Although I conversed mostly with Mr. and Mrs. Gardiner, I was situated so as to be able to glance surreptitiously at Miss Eliza. I caught her several times surveying the landscape, the stone bridge, the willows, the Spanish chestnuts, the glistening lake, the distant hills. Her eyes took on a dreamy quality then. My heart rejoiced. It seemed she was pleased with what she saw.

Georgiana arrived this afternoon. It has been her wish to meet Elizabeth for some time. I shall not make her languish. We shall go to Lambton tomorrow.

Georgiana

Pemberley, August 5

I must say my magical powers are increasing every week. I cannot take credit for making Miss Eliza appear at Pemberley, but my brother explained that that is exactly what happened.

We arrived yesterday, hardly had time to settle in and sleep, and today, Willy and Charles and I went to Lambton. Willy's impatience to have me meet *her* was surpassed only by mine, perhaps!

Well, what I can say after only a short meeting is that my brother has very good taste. The lady he has fallen in love with—I can definitely say it is love just by looking at him—is as wonderful a person as I would ever want for a friend. If not sister. In fact, now that I think of it, friend would be even better perhaps. Why let these men get in the way? Indeed, now that we have been acquainted, I feel I have every right to pursue the relationship on my own, establish a correspondence, and keep up the acquaintance in my own right, just in case my brother does silly things again.

Before he left for Pemberley, he and I had a fine, calm discussion where he confessed that he had asked for her hand in the most awkward and ridiculous fashion by pointing out that her social rank was unbelievably lower than his and that he was doing her a great favor by requesting the honor of matrimonial bliss with her. He didn't give a long explanation of all this; I had to extirpate it little by little. I might have laughed at his clumsiness, if I didn't know that it had caused him such pain. I did scold him a bit, and he said Fitzy was in perfect agreement with me!

Well, now I cannot blame her for refusing him. Whatever possessed him? He is always chiding me about reading novels, but if he had read just one or two, he would have known how it is done when you propose marriage. It must be done very romantically, by moonshine if possible, and invoke only love, love eternal!

At any rate, I liked her very well. I felt she had an uncommon understanding of situations, that she could gauge people's ideas and catch their meaning very swiftly, even if she did not know them.

I am impatient for their visit tomorrow, and for the day after tomorrow, when they shall dine with us here. I just wish Caroline and Louisa (and that awful Mr. Hurst) had not come down with us. I hope they do not spoil the fun.

Fitzwilliam Darcy

August 6

It is evening, and I have much to relate about the events of the day.

First, and most importantly, Georgiana and Miss Eliza seem to like each other very much.

As they stood together, I realized how much Georgiana has grown physically in the last year; she is definitely a few inches taller than Elizabeth, when I am quite certain that last July they were the same height. But she has grown in so many other ways. She is still a bit shy in company but composes herself more quickly than in the past, when necessary. These things, as Miss Eliza and my Aunt have said, take practice. Georgiana told me about practice. Practice! Everyone loves that word! I believe if dogs could talk, Gulliver would exhort me to practice.

I think I fell out of practice for many years. In my self-sufficiency and obnubilation, I decided I did not need to practice. I was well enough. I was perfect. I was tall, handsome (they say), well-educated, wealthy. I didn't need improving.

What a fool I was.

Well, I practiced today. I practiced conversing, smiling, including as many in the conversation as possible, wracking my brain for anecdotes. Elizabeth returned my efforts. We were all quite lively! Mr. and Mrs. Gardiner are of the genteelest sort in character, and they are worthy of further acquaintance. A year ago, I would have shunned them. *"Odi profanum vulgus et arceo…"* said Horace. I used to live by that saying. Now I see that perhaps Horace was being ironical. Now I see what an insufferable stance that is, to believe oneself above others due to one's wealth, and to avoid any contact with the undeserving.

Charles was as happy as anything to ask Miss Eliza about her sisters yesterday when we visited her in Lambton. As if he meant any but one…I believe that when she answered more specifically about Jane, her kind look in my direction meant that she no longer held such a grudge against me for my role in that sad situation. I know her expressions, and had she wanted to inflict pain or accusation, she would have been able to do it with just a glance. But she did not.

Today, I found that the more I forced myself to feel at ease, the more at ease I felt, and then I realized I did not need to force myself. I had regained a sort of happy sense of comfort with myself. I ignored all my former prohibitions, threw my cautious demeanor to the wind, and I saw with gratitude and joy that Miss Elizabeth, far from still feeding any resentment against me, seemed to have softened substantially toward me. Those smiles could not lie! And they thrust forward waves of pure joy in my heart! But can I allow myself to hope? Clearly, she is very well-mannered, and her pleasant demeanor fooled me at Rosings and may be fooling me now. But still…for some reason my heart was happy seeing her here today.

And now to give credit where credit is due: Georgiana is either a fairy or a witch. Perhaps I should have sought her advice years ago… The universe and my new disposition toward good may have turned the tide, as she predicted they would, if only I would quit my stubbornness. To her advice I owe my present glimpse into possible happiness.

But what a thorn to have Caroline among us today! At one point, when she and Charles were occupied in admiring a cushion cover that Georgiana had finished, Elizabeth came toward me and started saying, in very low tones and an air of seriousness, "Mr. Darcy, I must tell you—" but we were immediately interrupted by Caroline, who swooped upon us like a crow. The woman moves swiftly when she wants to!

"Miss Elizabeth," she cried. "I hear the militia have moved away from your little town of Meryton and are encamped in Brighton for the summer!"

"Yes, they have left, and…"

"What utter misery for *your* family," Caroline continued in that abominable sneering tone. "No officers to flirt with! What *can* your sisters be doing all day now? And you? I remember you ardently defending a certain officer… What was his name again…oh yes, Mr. Wickham."

Miss Elizabeth blanched, and Georgiana, who had approached our circle, let out a short cry. I was astonished and angry and did not know what stance to take. Silence hung. Bingley was looking at me with alarm. Georgiana was staring at Elizabeth.

"That is true," Elizabeth said calmly. "I did defend him."

Georgiana's color heightened. It seemed as if her eyes might fall out of her head, so hard was she staring at Elizabeth. She seemed about to speak but checked herself, as Elizabeth continued.

"But I had been ill-informed. I had heard false reports about him; but I have learned the truth and have since changed my mind. I can no longer defend any aspect of his character," Elizabeth said firmly.

My God. She had indeed read my letter. She had believed me. I silently prayed that she would not glance up at me, for I know not what she would have read in my countenance. She maintained eye contact with Caroline. I glanced at Georgiana. She looked very pale suddenly and was now staring at the floor. All this talk of Wickham must be so awful to her. After what he had tried to do. Any reminder would be sickening. I hated Caroline for inflicting this pain.

The woman did not quit. An evil smile darkened her features further, something I might have thought quite impossible. "You admit then, Miss Eliza, that my warnings to you last November were righteous, and that your scoffing at me was ill-founded?"

Bingley saved the situation from further awkwardness. In a stentorian voice, he declared, "Well, I must say I am still quite in the mood for music. Please, Caroline, will you indulge us, as we have put Miss Darcy to the task quite enough for this afternoon?"

I did not want Eliza and Georgiana pursuing the topic of George Wickham, so when I saw my sister looking quizzically and almost pleadingly at Eliza, I stepped in and engaged Georgiana on the flimsiest of topics. The visitors took their leave shortly afterwards, so I was able to prevent any private interview between them for the rest of the evening.

But frankly, who cares about Wickham? He is blessed with charm and good looks; he will surely find another heiress. Eliza must never have loved him. He will be out of my life soon.

I think back on my discussion with James in the coach, coming back from Rosings. Those three inexorable objections... Well, thanks to Caroline's indiscreet comments, I can now cross objection number two—Eliza's resentment toward me in the Wickham affair—off the list. Next, I shall soon make a full confession to Bingley and to Miss Eliza of my ugly interference in Bingley's affairs and my heartfelt contrition in that domain. That would take care of objection number one. And from the looks we exchanged today, I think I can believe that she does not hate me quite as much as she did before. But...not hating me is not what I want. I want her to love me as I love her.

Ah, what turmoil! I hope, and yet dare not hope. I do not know how I will ever fall asleep tonight.

August 7, Morning

I did fall asleep and slept like a rock for the first time in eons. It feels good to awake with a happy vision in one's head.

That vision was Miss Eliza's smile.

I have made up my mind. I will not let my bumbling manner in April and this misunderstanding about Wickham get in the way of my happiness, that of my sister, that of everyone at Pemberley. She refused me on the basis of a lie. In her innocence of the truth, she acted quite rationally, if a bit precipitously. But my wounded pride is happy to be overcome by the prospect of a lifetime of happiness with her.

I watched her walking about the rooms at Pemberley last night. She looked as though she belonged there.

How I love Pemberley! Pemberley has made everything right again. Eliza was not obsequiously fawning over its beauties, but I saw the glistening in her eyes and the softness of her smile while admiring the prospect toward the lake, the bridge, the woods, everything.

Mrs. Reynolds assured me that as per my habitual orders she had not shown the visitors the library, which satisfied me, for I want to be the one to take her there. I cannot wait to see her expression. It is said to be the best in all of Derbyshire.

I will go to Lambton today and study the situation. I must not let my brain be addled by the happy influence of Pemberley. I will very rationally converse with her and her aunt and uncle. Then, this evening, when they are here, somehow, I will find a way to speak privately with her. On the terrace…by the dragonfly pond…or in the rose garden, or perhaps by the ha-ha wall, or maybe even in the library! I will pay close attention, gauge every glance, assess every smile or frown, and perhaps I shall be able to sense whether she is amenable.

I am hopeful, but I am terrified. Am I capable of doing this, and could I ever survive a second rejection?

I have no choice. I must ask her, properly this time, to marry me.

August 7, Evening

What a difference a few hours make. When I last wrote in this journal, I was as happy as a lark. Now a somber emotion has taken hold of me. Not toward Elizabeth, no, on the contrary, my affection for her has redoubled. But toward that wretch, the miserable man that was nurtured in the bosom of Pemberley, only to ruin my happiness: George Wickham!

Thinking she was with her aunt and uncle, instead I found Miss Eliza quite alone at the Lambton Inn, in the most wretched condition. She had just received news from Miss Bennet that their sister Lydia, the tall gawkish one, had just fled from the protection of Col. and Mrs. Forster and run off! eloped! with none other than George Wickham! Elizabeth looked so miserable and choked with tears that I did not linger. One thing made me happy in all of this: she confided in me, and she readily declared that she believed every word in my letter concerning Wickham.

Georgiana was disappointed when I told her Miss Eliza and the Gardiners had been called back to Hertfordshire for a family emergency. I saw Caroline and Louisa exchanging snide expressions, and there was a glowing sense of triumph in the former's countenance as she expressed her heartfelt misery at being deprived of the company. Upon which she and Louisa settled at the piano for a loud duet.

I pretexted business letters to write and retired to my chamber, and here I will stay far away from those honking geese until supper.

Now I must lay down a plan to hunt down this piece of human trash and bring him to heel, once and for all.

August 8, Early Morning

Carruthers brought me not one, not two, but three letters, all from Pratt. They contained some news I wish I had received days ago, but of course they had all been directed to my house in town.

"Brighton, 28 July. Dear Sir, here are the latest news. I have had little to relate while the regiment was getting settled at Brighton, as for many weeks I was at my mother's side during her long illness; I returned to Brighton to find that just as in Meryton, G.W.'s presence causes quite a stir among the females of the species; he has carried on a couple of flirtations with daughters of well-to-do tradesmen, and he courts several girls at once at balls; quite the butterfly; but it all looks rather harmless, and I have noticed nothing very serious; however, since you lately asked that I keep you apprised of anything I could learn of anyone from Meryton and the environs, I must say that I have remarked that he is often seen with Lydia Bennet, of Longbourn, whose close friendship with Mrs. Forster I had already told you of and who is Mrs. Forster's special guest at Brighton; but so far, I have not been able to detect any marked interest on his part toward her.

"One evening last week, I had led him to drink a bit (not that he needs much encouragement from me), and when he started to loosen up again, I teased him about his success with the youngest ladies. To my surprise, he became a little angry with me and told me he was sick of their company and

was aiming for ladies of his own rank. As I expressed my doubt, he told me he was not just a commoner. He was "George Wickham of Pemberley." He said that as if he were the owner of the place. But of course, he was quite tipsy. Still, I thought I would inform you of this strange declaration, since it relates very particularly to you, Sir, and I know not what to make of it."

George Wickham of Pemberley! The snake! How dare he!!!
I took up the second letter. It was quite short, dated July 31:

"I am sending this forthwith, as there was an alarming incident yesterday. Having been at the bottle again (I do believe he is well on his way to becoming a complete drunkard, and I know he has already been reprimanded by his superior officer in that regard), G.W. talked about you particularly, Sir. I was prodding him, curious about his previous claim to being "George Wickham of Pemberley." He said that the current owner of Pemberley had only a slightly greater right to the title than he himself did, and that, were said current owner to pass, he, George Wickham, would be next in line. I thought I would inform you of this as quickly as possible."

I could not believe my eyes. I tore open the third letter. What other knavery would I witness now?

"August 2. Yesterday, George Wickham deserted. He was last seen waiting outside, a few streets from Marlborough House in Brighton, when a carriage stopped, into which he climbed. The driver, later questioned, said he had dropped three individuals off near St. Nicholas Church, where they had climbed into another coach en route for London. The driver said he had been hired by an old woman who had a much younger female companion with her. He described the older woman as having a pronounced limp and being extremely tall, over six feet. He had understood they were all kin, for the girl kept laughing about "her dear brother" as they climbed in. A curious detail he offered is that the two ladies had demanded that a flurry of blue ribbons be placed on the outside of the carriage. But, Sir, here is a material point, Wickham had left a note for me, which I have carried secretly ever since (not giving it to Colonel Forster), and which I will remit personally into your hands only, Sir, for it has to do with your family. I copy the important parts here for your perusal. "Pratt, as my loyal friend I tell you in secret that I am on my way to recovering my fortune in Pemberley. The mighty family that I had been forced away from has recognized my rights and is making amends for their past mistreatment. My sister and her governess shall fetch me, and we are to

be reunited. Pray explain to Colonel Forster that I shall return a wealthy man before the week is out." The young lady in the carriage, of course, was no sister of his; she has been identified as Miss Lydia Bennet, the intimate friend of Mrs. Forster. Mrs. Forster, as soon as Colonel Forster informed her of Wickham's desertion, produced a letter that everyone in Brighton now knows about (one should never underestimate the powers of servants), written to her by this Miss Lydia, announcing her love for G.W. and their plans for elopement. We are all rather surprised because he had said many times that although she pursued him relentlessly, he found her common, gawkish, and silly, and she has very little in way of a dowry."

I was dumbfounded. Not because Lydia had behaved in such a stupid manner, but because I recognized the older woman. Very tall, obvious limp. That is undoubtedly Mrs. Younge, whom I dismissed without referrals after her odious role in Georgiana's aborted elopement. What sort of witch is this woman? What wickedness prompts her to act in such evil ways!

But this only strengthens my resolve, and lightens my task, for it draws a clear line for my pursuit of the knave. Mrs. Younge will be very easily found out, as a limping six-foot female. I have every intention of dealing with her as harshly as I will deal with Wickham.

This very afternoon, I shall be on my way to London.

PART IV

Fitzwilliam Darcy

London, August 15

What a day! I am still unsettled; my brain will not let me rest. Although it is very late, I must, absolutely must, put all this in writing lest I get up in the morning and decide that these events did not occur.

I found the miscreants. It took longer than I had hoped, but when a man is liberal with coins, eventually tongues loosen. By process of elimination and frequent patronizing of coffeehouses, I narrowed my search down to a modest neighborhood near Fleet Street. The six-footer was soon identified, and my spies indicated a boarding house run by a widow, a Mrs. Shephard. A few hours of patient stalking, and finally I saw Mrs. Younge, returning from errands as the sun was setting.

I revealed myself to her just as she was about to enter the house. She let out a short cry and started shaking.

"Shall we go inside and have a talk, Mrs. Younge?"

"You…you have no right!" she croaked.

After I intimated that abducting a young girl of 15, of a good family, might bring her a lot of unpleasant consequences, she acquiesced. She showed me into a dark, stuffy parlor, lit a nasty tallow candle, and allowed her long limbs to fold and crash onto a settee. I remained standing.

"Where are they?"

"Upstairs. Room 2. She told me she was 20, I swear it."

"Tell me what your role has been in this."

"Why does a gentleman like you care that a silly girl is mad enough to pay me to get the man she wants?"

"Pay you?"

She nodded with an ugly smirk. "Money is not easy to procure, Mr. Darcy. You think it is easy to remake one's life? You dismissed me without references. You, high and mighty, though I had done nothing wrong, threw me out on the street. I was lucky enough that my sister took me in to help her run this establishment, but times are difficult."

I ignored her remark of having done nothing wrong. This was not the time to rehash last summer's unpleasantness at Ramsgate.

"How much did she pay you?"

"Two pounds."

"Two pounds! For two pounds you risked pursuit by the law, perhaps prison or the workhouse?"

She looked at me with pure hatred. "Yes, I know, for gentlemen like you two pounds is a trifle. For the rest of us, it might mean the difference between survival and starvation."

"So, she offered you two pounds to do what exactly?"

"I refuse to answer. You will not believe me. You will become violent. I heard you punched George."

I took a moment to quell my wrath. This woman was treading dangerous ground, but I needed to remain calm. "Yes, I did. He tried to abduct my sister! But you have nothing to fear. I have never laid a hand on a woman, and I never will."

"You will not report me to the authorities?"

"If you tell me the truth, no, I will not. I give you my word as a gentleman."

She snickered. "Hah! A gentleman! I know all about gentlemen! DARCY gentlemen!" She said the words as if they were poison she was spitting out.

"Mrs. Younge, I shall report you immediately unless you tell me everything. EVERYTHING! This establishment will be closed, and you and your sister will be out on the street." I must have looked menacing, because she shrank back, and she started shaking again.

"All right," she whispered. "What do you want to know?"

"What did she ask you to do, and how came you to know her?"

She was quiet a moment, then seemed to make up her mind. "I have been looking out for George for years. After you threw him out—" she saw my expression darken and faltered. "After he was er…left on his own, I had to look out for him. Last year, when I, like him, was…dismissed, I was able to communicate with him again."

"And…?"

"He wrote to me that he had joined the militia and was on his way to regaining respectability after his years of despair, that horrible pit of despair that he was driven to when he was…impoverished. Things got even better: he said that he had found a kind lady who had a bit of money and had agreed to marry him."

"Yes, go on."

"Then, about a month ago, he said he was in a bad way again. The young lady's family had made enquiries. They had found out he had been chased out of Pemberley. Had unpaid accounts in alehouses, gambling debts. The engagement was severed. He told me he had communicated with Miss Georgiana this summer…"

"Impossible!" I bellowed.

"I am sorry, but it is true…he showed me her letters."

"Forgeries, I am sure!" I exclaimed. She smirked and shook her head. I realized it was useless to argue with this hag. I still needed information. "So, then what?"

"Your sister promised George that she would help him. She was waiting for the right time. She said that she was trying to get you to understand the truth. But she couldn't. You wouldn't listen to her, or there were guests, or servants around, or you were up in town, or…one pretext after another. But then there were no more letters from her, and he fell into despair again. When his regiment came to Brighton, I was able to go there too, having saved a bit of money. The last few weeks, it's true, he has been drinking a lot. I would observe him, follow him. Once, I picked him up in the street, lying face down in his own sickness. I nursed him, cleaned him, had him brought back to camp surreptitiously, to avoid his getting into trouble."

"Exemplary charity," I muttered. "But where does Miss Lydia Bennet figure in all of this?"

"I was as faithful as a shadow to my George. He was coming to the point of self-destruction. I had to think for him, but I realized I would not be able to help him by myself. That broken engagement had made me think that what he needed was a young lady with real affection for him in her heart. I saw Miss Lydia pursuing him; they were not often alone, but even when they were in the company of other ladies and officers, I saw that she was as much in love with him as I've ever seen anyone."

"And him? Did he return the noble sentiment?"

"Not at all. He tried to dismiss her, once and again. I had my spies. But the girl is determined, high-spirited. I found out who she was. I befriended her. I encouraged her in her pursuit of him. I thought, if that other rich girl was too high and mighty for George, perhaps a girl like Lydia, with a little less money, but not completely destitute, would be better than nothing. A little affection, a little money. That is all he's ever wanted, you know," she said accusingly.

"So you encouraged her to pursue him? To raise his fortune?" This scheme sounded ridiculous to me.

"Yes. I found out she would have at least 50 pounds when her father died. Better than total destitution, and better than George getting court-martialed for striking an officer while drunk and then being executed—something I feared more than anything. Also better than being sent off to Bony's war fields, if we are to come to that."

"I'm sorry, but—why do you take so keen an interest in George Wickham?"

"Why should I tell you these private things?"

"Because, as I said, if you don't, I shall call the authorities forthwith and charge you with kidnapping, abduction, oh, I could produce quite a list." I spoke softly, but she could not mistake my serious tone.

She let out a long sigh that was almost a moan.

"Perhaps you know that I was in Mrs. Wickham's employ, many years ago."

"I had heard it said. So? You owe *him* nothing."

"No, perhaps not *him*. But I owed *her*. Because it was my fault."

"Her? Who? Your fault that what?"

The woman started weeping. I was disconcerted. I waited, with a horrible premonition of some awful revelation. But of a sudden, there was a commotion, voices and yelling in the hall, and hurried footsteps down the stairs. The door burst open, and there they were, George and Lydia, he looking sheepish and she rather disheveled. They stopped in their tracks. For a few seconds, there was not a sound but Mrs. Younge's unabated but soft sobbing.

Then Lydia cried, "Mr. Darcy!!! what the devil are *you* doing here? Look, Wicky! It's Mr. Darcy!"

George turned on his heels to flee, but I caught him by the elbow.

"Wickham, one more step and I demolish your face."

Lydia started laughing hysterically. "My darling Wickham, you see Mr. Darcy does not want you to go out tonight any more than I do!"

George said nothing. His arm felt soft and rubbery under my grip, and he did not fight.

"Miss Bennet, pray gather your things, I am to take you to your aunt Gardiner's," I said sternly.

She pouted. "Oh no, I am not leaving my Wickham. Mr. Darcy, have you seen my sisters lately? What do they think of this? Do they know I am Mrs. Wickham? We have eloped! You see me a married woman!" She twirled about in the dank, nasty parlor, her long loose hair flying.

I still had Wickham in a deathly tight vise. He politely asked that I unhand him, and as he seemed rather subdued, I did, cautiously, and he went to sit by Mrs. Younge, looking rather bored. In fact, he yawned.

"Married? I don't believe it. Who performed the ceremony?" I asked. "Wickham, is this true?"

"Miss Lydia says a Catholic priest from France did the deed. I have no recollection." His tone was strangely flat. Mrs. Younge had stopped sobbing and now she started cackling. One of the two miserable candles sputtered and went out, and we were left in a strange chiaroscuro of wild shadows. Lydia went to sit on George's knee and played with his hair, singing softly, while he ignored her. I felt I had penetrated into an underworld of madness.

"Yes, Père François married them as soon as we arrived in London, and I and my sister were witnesses. Right here in this parlor," Mrs. Younge pronounced with authority.

I stared at the silent, passive George. I needed to talk with him in private, and I needed to get Lydia out of there. Begrudgingly, Mrs. Younge condescended to call for an errand boy. I quickly scribbled a note to Mr. Gardiner, with whom I had communicated shortly after arriving in London. I was not going to leave until Lydia was in safe hands.

In a few minutes, Wickham seemed to rouse himself from his stupor. "Mrs. Younge, could we trouble you for a pot of tea?" he pronounced slowly. "Mr. Darcy must be rather thirsty." Mrs. Younge rose, reminding me of a sickly old heron, curtsied in the most awkward fashion, and left the room.

"Miss Bennet," I began.

"Mrs. Wickham!" she corrected indignantly.

"Miss Lydia," I continued, "have you any idea what your family has been going through in the last two weeks? Do you realize what you've done?"

"Aye, I've done what none of my sisters have done, and I'm the youngest!" she exclaimed. "It is too droll!"

"Your mother is in hysterics, your sisters are devastated, your father is in shock. You did not bother to communicate with them. Whether you have been married by this French cleric or not, in the eyes of society you are not married. Banns were not published, I suppose no special license was had, and only two not very credible witnesses would attest to this union. Even your so-called husband does not seem quite sure of what happened. Therefore, I ask that you go quietly with your uncle when he comes to fetch you, for the sake of your family."

"La! A new bride does not leave her beloved husband like that on their honeymoon," she cried.

We argued a bit more, her absurdities a perfect foil for my most reasonable exhortations. Mrs. Younge returned with tea. I abstained, but Wickham drank the steaming beverage avidly. I dismissed Mrs. Younge, telling her I would speak with her later.

Lydia was uncontrollable. I remonstrated and tried to reason until I thought I would gladly have strangled her. I was concerned that I might never extirpate her from the boarding house, except by force, and that would cause a scandal. She was dismissive, insolent, very pleased with herself, flitting about, making lascivious jokes, and spouting amorous platitudes to her dear Wickham. Wickham had a strange, flat smile and dead eyes, as if he was not even hearing or seeing her.

Finally, to my great relief, Mr. Gardiner arrived. He did not acknowledge Wickham's presence. Nor were there any effusions between the niece and the uncle, nor did he find it useful to scold her. I understand she is not a great favorite of his. Mrs. Gardiner, he said, was waiting in the carriage, and he was ready to take Lydia and her things forthwith. Lydia started weeping. "You can't take me away from my husband. I am a married woman."

"Now tell the truth, Lydia," Mr. Gardiner said gently, glancing at me as if to say he had a plan. "Did you have a splendid wedding, a proper one, with all your friends and sisters seeing you in your best attire? with music and candles and cake and wine and flowers?"

"Oh Lordy, no! It was a nasty affair in a dark place—well, right here, if you can believe it—with a short fat French popish priest who could hardly speak English!"

"I believe, if you come with me now, I have it on good authority that your mother has planned a good and proper ceremony for you. With new wedding clothes and a great feast with *blanc de veau* and white soup. Wedding cake and wine for all of Meryton."

"Oh!" Lydia beamed. Mr. Gardiner stole another glance at me. I nodded slightly, grateful for his skill. "Well, I do want all my friends and sisters to see me and my Wicky, for sure. Kitty will be green with jealousy! She will sob and moan forever!" She laughed and kissed Wickham on the mouth. "But why must I leave my Wickham?"

"Your aunt must take you to the best warehouses of London for your trousseau and dress! She has made appointments to go with you early tomorrow morning. It will be much easier if you come with us tonight."

The temptation was too great. "You will not mind, my love?" she asked Wickham.

He shook his head slowly, not looking at her. Mrs. Younge was called back in and asked to go upstairs to gather Lydia's things. Meanwhile the girl covered her darling Wicky with noisy kisses, made many pledges, and my relief was profound when Mr. Gardiner took the girl away.

I was now alone with Mrs. Younge and George. He seemed to snap out of his dreamlike trance after Lydia left. Strangely, he ignored me and addressed Mrs. Younge.

"Why did you do this to me?" he asked in a low, pained tone.

"Dear George, I had to save you from yourself," she said, pleadingly.

"It was not right. You tricked me. You said that it would be Georgiana. Instead, I find this little chit."

I jumped. "Georgiana? Again? What has she to do with this?"

"Everything," Wickham replied. In a halting voice, he proceeded. "Mrs. Younge said Georgiana was coming. To save me. She gave me a short note from Georgiana. It said to wait at the appointed place. If I saw a carriage adorned with blue ribbons, it would be her. I waited for the carriage. I climbed in. Two persons were inside, they had their faces concealed, but I recognized Mrs. Younge. I started talking to Georgiana. At least, I thought it was Georgiana. Mrs. Younge told me to hush. The carriage took off at great speed. They gave me a draught of something like small beer to drink. I don't remember anything after that, just waking up in a bed upstairs, with Lydia by my side."

Wickham put his head in his hands and was rocking slowly. "Georgiana was going to save me, right the wrongs that have been done to me. She was going to take me to Pemberley. Instead I found myself with Lydia Bennet, in a bed, in a creaking and stuffy boarding house, in London. Did you write that note, Mrs. Younge, imitating Georgiana's handwriting?"

I looked at Mrs. Younge. She was studying the dirty floor with great attention. Clearly, she was as guilty as the day was long.

"You keep bringing up wrongs, Wickham," I said harshly. "But you brought those wrongs upon yourself. All your life. If you recall, you were dissolute at school."

"Many young men are, and I had good reason. Do you know what it is like to not know who you are? To hear some things, to be told one thing and be told otherwise by others, and float through life untethered?"

He sounded insane. I continued.

"*You* decided to give up the living and took the sum of money instead."

"I needed the cash immediately, to pay debts."

"And last year, you tried to seduce Georgiana and run away with her, and force a marriage, for her fortune! And now you were trying to do the same again!" I said, my tone rising.

"No! NO! Those were not at all my intentions. I never thought of her in that way. Even a knave like me knows you don't marry your sister!"

"WHAT?" I was flabbergasted. For a while, no one said anything. Mrs. Younge's head started bobbing up and down, up and down, as if to lend her agreement. Then, George started talking composedly, deliberately. Words that pierced my soul.

"My intention, at Ramsgate last year, was simply to provide to Georgiana some time alone with me and Mrs. Younge, so that together we could explain to her, without shocking her too much, what Mrs. Younge has known all her life and had only just revealed to me. That the late Mr. Darcy, your father, was my father."

I was speechless. George and I both looked at Mrs. Younge. She finally raised her eyes and told her story calmly. As a young woman, maid to Mrs. Wickham, she had been tasked with facilitating the goings on between Mr. Darcy and Mrs. Wickham. "There were but two of us in on the secret. My husband, now dead, and me. Old Mr. Wickham would be sent for weeks at a time on errands in Scotland, and Mr. Darcy would come to the hunting lodge and meet Mrs. Wickham there. Mr. Younge, as forester, played the lookout, and I prepared the lodge and then erased all traces of their passage. It was wicked, but I was young, and what choice do servants have? We do as we are told. But she died, and it was all my fault. Without my help, they could never have…" She stopped and breathed hard for a few seconds.

"It was on your account, Mr. Darcy," she continued in a labored voice. "Not your fault, but because of you. You may not know that your mother had lost three boys before you. Your birthing was so long, so terrible, and your mother was left so weak afterwards, that the midwife and the doctor both absolutely forbade any more children."

"Impossible! How do you explain Georgiana's birth then?" I asked.

"Your mother knew that Mr. Darcy was seeking attention elsewhere. Mrs. Wickham had died giving birth to George, when you were not yet two. I was with her when she died. She told me she was happy because she had given a son to the man she loved. Those were her words exactly: "I die happy because I have given a son to the man I love." I never spoke of it, I swear it, but your mother—Mrs. Darcy—must have guessed what happened. And she was deathly afraid that your father, following nature's urges, would go elsewhere again after Mrs. Wickham's death. Her pride rebelled. When she felt strong enough again, she insisted that they resume life as husband and wife. But fate was harsh; she had three more miscarriages, and then, at last, the little miracle of Georgiana appeared. The birth was difficult, again, and it left her extremely weak and she never quite recovered. She died, as you know, when Georgiana was still an infant. But you were a lad, in town with your tutor then, and they just told you that she took ill. The truth is, that child killed her, just like you, Mr. George, killed your poor mother. And your father, Mr. George, was never the same after his beloved Eleanor died. He lingered a few more years. Poor Mr. Wickham."

I felt as though someone had punched me in the stomach. My breathing was rapid and shallow. For some reason, although I hated every word she spoke, I believed the woman.

Everything I had taken as God's truth was a lie. My good, wonderful, revered father? A scoundrel. My mother, a victim. My own existence, the cause of such sorrow and pain. And Georgiana, pretty, happy Georgiana, the cause of her mother's death. I had been told Mrs. Wickham had been a frivolous woman who spent away the little money her husband had. I had been told…oh, so many things, but not that my boyhood companion, whom I had loved in my youth and despised later, was my brother.

I felt their eyes on me, and to my astonishment, their looks were of pity rather than resentment. I told them I needed to study this situation and I would return on the morrow or two days' hence. I took leave rather hastily, my brain reeling with the revelations.

I do not want to believe any of this, but my inner soul recognizes the truth.

As I have been putting all this down to paper, a thousand memories and details come to me to corroborate the veracity of this story. The many times strangers took us for brothers when we were young. That expression in my father's eyes sometimes when looking at George. And my mother's penetrating glance, studying George's features as a boy. And now I understand that what I had interpreted as depression and melancholy in her was not a mental deficiency but the result of her difficulties in childbearing, and all the consequences of that on the family. And now my father's last request, that I should be mindful of George, becomes crystal clear. Of course, he could not confess the truth to me.

How could I have not seen it before?

I have been shaken to the core.

I still have many questions, and one of them is Georgiana's role in trying to help George. Both he and Mrs. Younge kept referring to Georgiana as a kind of savior. Mrs. Younge said George received letters from her. This is unaccountable. She couldn't possibly have sent these letters secretly. But why would they lie about that? And now I think back on her strange questions, her intrepid pursuit of odd conversations with me in the last few months. Her asking me if I would like to have a brother. And I think back on Ramsgate. I recall what Georgiana told me when I joined her unexpectedly there. She never did say she was going to *elope* with George. She told me she had to tell me something about him, that she loved him so much…and I interrupted her in horror. But she never did say she was *in love* with him. I jumped to that conclusion. My bellowing voice scared her…she could not speak for tears. I panicked and sent her home immediately.

And Mrs. Younge…when I dismissed her, I truly believed her to be lying. She implored me to listen to her, but I didn't. I did violence to them both. I was despotic, unfeeling, and arrogant. In that respect, how right Elizabeth was. Alas, she is more lost to me now than ever, if ever she finds out—and she inevitably will—that her sister Lydia's disgrace was partly, if unwittingly, caused by me.

I have been so blind.

August 16

I went back to the boarding house today. I had schooled myself: since I was to blame for much of this situation, I would listen and do the best I could for all parties concerned, even if it cost me the opprobrium of society.

As a first step toward my newfound contrition, I had agreed to have a calm discussion and dinner with George and Mrs. Younge. Mrs. Shepard had prepared a good meal for us, and I had procured some wine. With Lydia Bennet safely away and a calmer atmosphere, George sounded more coherent. The wine helped me.

As soon as Mrs. Shepard was finished serving us and left, I asked Mrs. Younge if anyone else (beside my mother) at Pemberley had ever suspected the truth. At first, she said she doubted it, for the tryst did not last very long. "A few months. She was with child almost immediately, I believe. And once that was established, Mr. Darcy never returned to her." But I sensed some hesitation in her.

"And you are quite sure?"

"Well…there was one night, when I was accompanying Mrs. Wickham back to her lodging, when I suspect we were seen by someone. A light was shining in the woods, but was quickly extinguished. She was quite alarmed, but I reasoned it must be a poacher, and didn't think about it much until later, when some people started saying things about George."

"Do you think Mr. Wickham ever knew?"

"I cannot tell. But I suspect that Mrs. Prescott, the midwife—you know she is Mrs. Annesley's cousin—I suspect that she knew, for she had said something very strange a few days after George was born."

"Which was…?"

"That in all her years she had only seen two babies with a sixth finger on each hand and that those boys were probably related. She had just tied off the vestigial ones from little George."

"And the other boy was me, I suppose, 18 months earlier."

"Exactly so."

As if to further corroborate our fraternal ties, George and I happened to look at the sides of our little fingers, exactly at the same time, to check that the almost imperceptible nubs were still there. I felt myself blushing at our identical reactions. Mrs. Younge attempted a smile, but it came out like a grimace. She continued, "And both Mr. and Mrs. Wickham had brilliant blue eyes, and she told me later that she had never seen two blue-eyed parents bring forth a brown-eyed child. And other people suspected things. I know George was teased when he was a bit older, by other boys in the village, about being a bastard child. I am sorry," she said quickly, the vile word having found their mark. George suddenly had a horribly pained expression.

I, of course, had been shielded from any gossip. No one had ever called me a bastard. I had had a happy, carefree childhood, well sheltered in Pemberley. I was the legitimate son and heir.

I had to begin the unsavory task of making amends. "Well, George," I said, "all I can say is that I am very sorry if I have caused you pain over the years. And I am especially sorry that we came to blows and that I punched you last year at Ramsgate."

"I can understand your behavior, as long as you were ignorant of all this, but why did you not at least inquire after the truth after I sent you that letter?"

"Letter?"

"Yes. Last September. I know you received it. Did you not believe anything I wrote? I pleaded with you. I explained what my intentions had been when you misunderstood what happened at Ramsgate. I explained that Mrs. Younge had revelations about our kinship. Did you think me mad?"

I remembered then my angry gesture after Carruthers had remitted the letter to me. My throwing of the polluting papers, unread, into the fire. My hatred, anger, and resentment had not permitted me even to entertain the possibility that I might not be in full command of the truth.

The truth. Well, I had to use the truth as my guiding star from now on, and so I told George what I had done with the letter. "I am sorry for that. It was very wrong of me. Please accept my apology."

He sighed. "Well, it's better than having read it and THEN ignored it." He smiled at me, and for the first time I saw my father's eyes in his face. He is a good-looking man; no wonder Miss Elizabeth felt an attraction. But now was not the time to think of *that*.

"I want to improve your situation. Though by law you have no claim to anything in Pemberley because of illegitimacy, in my eyes I think you are due some redress. But what are we to do about Miss Lydia Bennet? By now, all of her relations and all of Meryton probably know that you eloped."

He put his head in his hands. "Is there any way out of this for me without marrying her?"

Mrs. Younge intervened. "You have been married by Père François."

"I was drugged. Not in possession of my faculties." He gave Mrs. Younge a bitter look.

I continued: "The point is that she has been compromised. She is as good as unmarriageable by anyone but you. And since marriages not performed by a prelate of the Church of England are not valid, you must be married properly."

"The laws of our society are ridiculous."

"And yet we cannot circumvent them. I am sorry to be blunt, but have you… uhh… consummated the bonds…?"

His silence, followed by a long sigh, was eloquent.

"Then, I am afraid there is no other solution. Mrs. Younge, I thank you for speaking the truth, but you acted extremely rashly and possibly criminally in the aiding of the abduction and drugging of Mr. Wickham, and taking away from her guardian a girl who is not yet sixteen."

She looked at me with alarm. "I swear she told me she was 20!"

As Miss Lydia was not in my eyes a beacon of moral rectitude, I believed Mrs. Younge.

"But you did drug George?"

She started weeping. "It was not supposed to knock him out for so long! It was only supposed to last for a few hours, so that we would be well on our way to Gretna Green before he discovered that the girl was not Georgiana! But he became extremely ill, and so we had to stop in London. He was alive and yet like dead! He was asleep yet looking awake. He spoke, he walked. But all his talk was nonsense, as in a dream. He would see things that were not there. He was sick several times. And then he would lose consciousness altogether for hours at a time."

I was appalled. "Where on earth did you procure this potion?"

"That, you will excuse me if I refuse to tell. And what does it signify now? Anyway, when I thought he might be dying, I brought him here and called in a priest I knew. A very good person, from a fine, wealthy French family. Escaped during the Terror. Père François asked for the history of all of this, found out they were in the same room, and insisted on marrying them forthwith."

"And Miss Lydia had no idea that her groom was in a stupor?"

"I think she is in a dream world of her own, to tell the truth," she said, somewhat bitterly. "I did not count on her being as flighty and silly as all that. But it was 'dear Wickham' here and 'dear Wickham' there, and she was very excited about being married, said it would make her mamma so happy and her sisters so jealous."

I did recognize there a fair portrait of the damsel. If only there had been no consummation…there would be ways to hush it up. But what if she were already with child? We could not risk it.

George and I discussed it, and George did the unbelievable. He accepted to get married, or stay married, God knows which, to Lydia. "I will do what is right by her. If we are married, so be it. Dame Fortuna's wheel turns, and I am an optimist: my stars must rise from here on. Lydia is not so very horrid."

"You called her a chit yesterday."

"Did I? But that potion is now starting to wear off. I am thinking more clearly… I believe Lydia realized the powers of the potion, and that she has been administering it to me in small doses all this time."

"Oh, no!" Mrs. Younge cried. Clearly, this was a powerful drug, and Lydia had been happy with its effects.

"Last night," Wickham continued, "a few hours after Lydia left, I felt my mental powers returning to me a bit, at last, and this morning I was thinking if it had to come to this—to marriage—it would not necessarily be unbearable. Though she would never have been my first choice, Lydia is not unattractive, not stupid, and she is very good-humored; her affection for me is beyond the norm, and she is so young there is still a possibility of her maturing a bit in the next few years."

I was skeptical. When I mentioned that returning to Col. Forster's regiment was quite out of the question, given the scandal, he expressed interest in quitting England altogether and going to Canada as soon as possible. "The land is young and immense. With my new wife, we will make our own life there, far away from bonnet makers, balls, landed gentry," here he flashed that winning smile at me, "and village gossips. And that infernal mother of hers!"

I had to laugh. We were brothers indeed.

"Are you quite sure?" I asked.

"I made my decision that I would seek my fortune abroad after Miss King broke off our engagement. But I had thought about it for a long time. For more than ten years now, really, I have been seeking a new world, a new life. This old England with its crusty traditions bores me. In my youth," he added, looking rather intently at me, "I heard tales of Canada that filled me with longing for the vast forests and glittering lakes and rivers. It was in fact a relief when Miss King dismissed me. Had we married, I would be imprisoned in this circuit of social engagements. I decided to go, and so I will. The only difference is that now, I will have a companion."

I still had my doubts, but I applauded his decision. We discussed things further, and it was agreed that they should officially marry here, in a proper church, within the bosom of the good Church of England, with Lydia's uncle and aunt in attendance. Then, they should return to Longbourn and thereafter go stay in the north until they could secure passage to the colonies. I decided a large sum of money, more than twice what he had been given before instead of the living, might lighten his burden (as well as my vague but nagging sense of guilt). At first, he refused such an "enormous sum," but I like to have my way, and he soon acquiesced.

George and I discussed the extent to which any of this should be revealed. He said he did not want the word bandied about that he was the illegitimate son of a wealthy man and his steward's wife. He didn't want his mother's memory soiled. On my side, I did not want my father's faults to be known. So, in principle, the story is that George and Lydia were discovered by Mr. Gardiner, George was planning to marry her from the start but took extremely ill before they could even depart for Gretna Green, they are in love, they are now married, and Mr. Gardiner arranged it all.

My feelings tonight are mixed. I am in fact, unexpectedly, happy to have a brother—this is very odd, but the burden of being the only son seems to have been lifted from my shoulders—and I am also relieved to see him leave soon. My anger, my hatred of him, which poisoned my peace for so long, all of it has evaporated, and I can breathe, I can finally breathe, as I haven't done in a twelvemonth. But I am also still deeply shocked by my father's behavior. How little we know those closest to us! My father, my hero. How could he have done such a thing?

On a happier note, I am relieved to think that Miss Eliza can no longer hold the charge of cruelty against me. And yet, I am miserable in knowing that she shall never know it.

August 31

Today Lydia Bennet officially became Mrs. Wickham in the Church of England. She was very angry at first, Mrs. Gardiner said, because we had tricked her into leaving her dear Wicky by making her believe the wedding would take place in Meryton with all her friends in attendance. But Mrs. Gardiner invoked excellent pretexts regarding difficulties owing to banns and licenses, and after she took her to warehouses, bought her all sorts of clothing and a trousseau (with money I had provided), the bride was happy enough.

I took the opportunity to speak to Lydia in private just before the ceremony. In the sternest tones I told her that she was not to breathe a word of my presence here to anyone. Not to her mother, not to her sisters, not to her aunt Phillips in Meryton, not to officers or friends, not to her dear Mrs. Forster. Nobody. I made her promise several times, and she did, but somewhat nonchalantly. She was more interested in exclaiming upon how handsome her husband was, and how silly it was to have to marry twice, and if it could be twice, why not do it again in Meryton for a third time. How droll that would be!

I wonder how George will manage her in the wilds of Canada.

I hope she remembers her promise. I would be mortified if Eliza learned the truth. But also, I wish she could.

Right after the nuptials, before the newlyweds left for Hertfordshire, I took George aside.

"When I was still at Netherfield, Miss Elizabeth seemed to know something of your past. Do not think that I am angry, but please, what did you tell her about our history?"

George turned a bit red. "Well, I did not tell the absolute truth, and I was so angry at you for ignoring my pleas, and all that I had written in my letter, that I painted you to be rather a villain, willfully ignoring your father's wishes and refusing me that living. I had just learned a few months previously, definitively, about the truth of my birth… I felt victimized. Your silence I read as contempt and hatred. It addled my thinking, and I told her a few lies, and I did tell her that your father liked me very much, perhaps more than he did you. Which certainly was not true."

"I see." It was depressing to think that *that* last bit might indeed be true. If he had in fact loved Mrs. Wickham, would my father not have felt a special affection for their child, the little boy who would carry her memory?

"But I shall tell her the truth about everything as soon as possible," he declared.

"There is no need. In fact, I ask you, for my sake, to tell her nothing. One truth would lead to another, and we have already decided that our parents' reputations need not be soiled. I have already told Miss Eliza Bennet my side of the story, which of course was very incomplete and wrong, and I shall be the one to tell her that there was a misunderstanding and that there is in fact little blame to be placed at your feet with regards to my sister."

"I am at your service, Fitzwilliam," he said. "I will do as you say."

But speaking of Georgiana, there was one more point that needed clarification: those letters that both Mrs. Younge and George had talked about. Although now I believed Mrs. Younge and George to be sincere, I could not accept that Georgiana would engage in a surreptitious correspondence, in blatant disregard of my orders. I was about to ask him to clarify that point, when Lydia—Mrs. Wickham—came prancing toward us and caught her husband's arm.

"Come, come, Mr. Wickham! Husband! My sisters await, my mother awaits, the Lucases, hah! yes, the Lucases await! Lord, how happy I am! I am one year younger than Maria and married before her! Oh, that Mrs. Lucas gloated so much when Charlotte snatched that awful Mr. Collins from Lizzy. He was distractedly in love with Lizzy first, you know! Followed her around the house like a puppy, it was quite droll! Well, now I am married before Maria! Before any of my sisters! Let's go and be merry. Goodbye, Mr. Darcy!"

Off they went, and with them my last chance to hear from George what had been his dealings with Georgiana these last six months.

September 1

I had the pleasure of dining with the Gardiners twice while all these events were taking place. Mr. Gardiner is a fine man, with excellent understanding, and we veered off the ponderous topics of Lydia and marriage laws to discuss more interesting things. It is a pity that we might never meet again. I was quite careful not to mention Elizabeth too much, though I did ask after her out of civility, and his praise of his favorite niece quite matched my impressions.

I did not tell Mr. Gardiner the truth about George.

I went back to Mrs. Shepard's boarding house. I had acted badly toward Mrs. Younge when I imperiously dismissed her, and my reparation has been to apologize and to promise her a faithful yearly sum for her to live on. She colored a bit, thanked me, and said, "You are a gentleman, sir. And despite what I said earlier, I believe your father was one too. Even after what happened."

How easy it is to soothe souls when one has a little money. I have never thought too much about the depth of power that was given to me with my fortune, and here again I have been remiss.

So. My list of reparations continues. Now that George and Mrs. Younge are settled, I have to make a contrite confession to Charles. He is coming tomorrow, and I shall immediately set upon the business at hand.

Georgiana

Pemberley, September 1

Willy has written to me. He says that his business in town is concluded (that is welcome news), but that now he has other business, something to do with Charles Bingley, in the country—he did not say where. These have been strange events, meeting Miss Eliza and then having our dinner abruptly canceled, Willy acting absolutely deranged, pretexting urgent business in town, and leaving the next day, when he had only just arrived from town a few days before. Well, I am glad if everything has been fixed now. I wonder if Mr. Bingley and my brother are going back to the house in Hertfordshire.

But Willy wrote something else, and I find it a little frightening. He says he has news about George and that it is good news, and that I should not worry, but we will need to talk about it.

I dread what that news might be, given Willy's dogged resentment against George for many years and the fact that he forbade me to even mention his name, ever since that awful time at Ramsgate. He might think I am afraid of George being predatory again. Or maybe he thinks I am in love with him. Ah, that makes me smile. I do need to talk seriously with my brother, but sometimes he intimidates me.

I wish Miss Eliza would come, just all by herself, to visit *me*.

Fitzwilliam Darcy

Netherfield, September 2

In the blessed absence of his sisters, Bingley returned to Netherfield with me today. The servants had prepared the place with so much attention that it looked very much like it did when we quit it abruptly—on my orders—almost a year ago. On my *suggestion* this time, we returned: I pretexted that we should get a little sport there, as he is an avid shooter. I really wanted to see for myself the depth of his feelings toward Miss Bennet, and of hers toward him. And let us not fool ourselves. I wanted an opportunity to see Elizabeth again. My philanthropy toward Charles was tainted with a bit of self-interest. Well, so be it. Perfection is not my goal anymore; happiness is.

I decided against making my confession to Bingley while we were still in town. It seemed more fitting that he should be closer to the object of his affections. I should mend things in the place where I had broken them.

And so, as we walked along a brook that used to be one of my favorite haunts, I confessed all. I started by saying I was a busybody, a fool, an imbecile, and was not worthy of his friendship. He laughed boyishly. "Darcy, this is a novel stance! What have you to accuse yourself of?" he asked.

"I did something unpardonable. I lied to you."

"Did you now?" He looked surprised but not too worried. "About what?"

"About Miss Bennet."

He lost his insouciant demeanor. "What do you mean?"

"I told you I thought she did not care for you. Although the first time I said that, I believed it somewhat, on later occasions I was deliberately deceiving you."

"Deceiving me? But why?"

"You are too good, Charles. You would not understand the depravity and superficiality of my character. I was a coward and a bully. I was afraid her family was unsuitable, not good enough for me to frequent, and I hated to lose your society because of that, and so I made up a narrative to detach you from Miss Bennet."

Charles was silent. I was feeling very uncomfortable. At length he spoke.

"But you really thought her affection for me was not very strong."

"I had no business having any thought or opinion on the matter. I was an arrogant pompous fool to direct your life in that way, and I ask you to forgive me."

He smiled sadly. "Perhaps I am the fool, to be so easily guided by my best friend. But I suppose Miss Bennet is now the object of much attention by other men. I assume she has quite forgotten me."

"I have it on good authority that she has not forgotten you, that she admits no courting by any other man, and that her affection for you is still as strong as ever and stronger than you may suspect."

"You jest with me, Darcy."

"I have more to confess. She came up to town this winter, stayed three months, and though she called at the Hursts' and wrote to Caroline several times, Caroline and I concealed her presence there from you."

For the first time, I saw a gleam of real anger in Charles's eyes. "You did *what*? How could you? And you call yourself my friend? And Caroline…? My God! The number of times I asked Caroline if she had had any communication from Miss Bennet—and each time, she said 'No, not a word'—She was lying to me?"

"Yes, it was a concerted effort. We feared for you, but we were very much in the wrong. I am ashamed of myself. Miss Bennet did uphold her end of the acquaintance, but Caroline dropped it."

"Well. I shall have a talk with Caroline. This is intolerable. From now on, she can stay with Louisa." He kicked a tree, picked up small stones and threw them violently into the brook, muttering imprecations. Frankly, I would not have been surprised if he had hurled a large rock toward my face.

"Please do not be too angry with her. I am most to blame."

He seemed calmer after his physical exertions. He came right up to me.

"Darcy. Tell me the truth. How do you know Miss Bennet still likes me?"

"Her sister Elizabeth told me so quite frankly in April. Told me that Jane Bennet loves you."

"Loves me!"

"And then in August, you recall Miss Eliza visited Pemberley, and in private she reiterated that fact to me."

"And still you said nothing to me…all this time…all those times when I opened up to you about my inability to forget Miss Bennet this winter, this spring, you had the gall…the audacity…the presumption…to LIE to me?"

"Yes. I am ashamed of my conduct. I don't know what came over me. I beg your forgiveness."

"I shall give that due consideration." His tone was lightening. The clouds on his face were clearing.

"One thing is certain. Miss Bennet is in love with you. She loves you with all her heart. She has always loved you, and she loves you still."

His happy smile made me truly ashamed of having been so deceitful with him. "Tell me, Darcy, do you think she still likes me today, this very minute? Because, you know, we are only three miles from Longbourn. A few minutes on horseback. And if you think that she has not quite forgotten me, for your punishment, I request that you accompany me there forthwith!"

We raced like schoolboys across the field and slowed to a walk only when we might be seen by servants. The old English decorum. For a fleeting second, I was envious of George's prospects, forging a new life in a wild, vast land across the ocean, far from the prying eyes of society and servants. But then I thought of his wife. And of the wife I might have, if only I could win her love. And then I was not envious anymore.

London, October 2

Well, it's been a long, lonely month. I am glad that my meddling did not destroy Charles' chance for happiness. A few days after I left Netherfield, I received a short, incoherent letter from him retelling his happy prospects and the perfections of his betrothed. I was not surprised at his bubbling joy, but it reinforces my pain. I cringe as I reflect upon how dastardly my interference was; I am horrified by my behavior, my pretexts, my excuses, my self-serving reasoning, my superior stance. I cannot reproach myself enough for thinking it was my duty to direct his life. Especially when it is apparent that I cannot even direct my own.

For I find myself as hopelessly separated from Eliza Bennet as I have ever been.

When we first went to Longbourn that day, after I had made my full confession to Charles, there was awkwardness on everyone's part. Elizabeth hardly looked at me; she sat rather stiffly, engrossed in her work, which I know is not her habit, though she did inquire with civility about my sister. I was confused by her taciturnity and found it difficult to return to the happier feelings and easiness that I believed we shared when I last saw her at Pemberley.

How much I should like to explain to her everything that happened with George and Lydia! But that is quite impossible. In fact, I could find no opening for even light conversation, and I was increasingly perplexed by her lack of spirits every time we went to Longbourn. I could swear that at Pemberley, before the unfortunate news of the elopement, she seemed well-disposed toward me. Am I still so completely incapable of reading a woman's mind?

Perhaps she is under the mistaken impression that now, with this marriage, which would make George Wickham her brother, I will have nothing to do with her…and little does she know that he already is (and has always been) *my* brother, even though on the wrong side of the bed, as wags would say. She thinks I abhor him. I once did, I admit that, but now that is quite over. However, I will never be able to tell her the truth.

Perhaps we are separated forever, for I do not know how to break the impasse of my doubts as to her true feelings toward me.

To whom could I turn? I cannot ask Bingley to discreetly ask Jane to discreetly ask Elizabeth… I must think like Georgiana and trust that somehow, someday, if I nurture enough hope, something will happen, some cosmic beneficence will trigger celestial events whereby her feelings will be made clear to me. And so, I hold on to my dream.

Hah. I had my chance, and it slipped between my fingers. I am a dunce and a fool.

Georgiana

Pemberley, October 4

Well, here I am like last year, alone again in Pemberley. I am not to return to town until Christmas. No music teacher has been found here. I have been so bored and anxious since leaving London, I have had nothing to write about.

But today I received a letter from Willy, the first in a rather long time. What interesting news! First, my brother writes that Charles Bingley is engaged! and to none other than Elizabeth Bennet's sister Jane!

Well, if this Miss Jane is as lovable as Miss Eliza, I am very happy for him, and I need not worry anymore that Willy would want me with Charles!

But the most shocking part of his letter concerns George. It seems he is now married, to none other than the *youngest* of the Bennet sisters. Her name is Lydia, and she is my age. I suppose they have been in love for a while, and perhaps that is why George stopped communicating with me, why he broke off the engagement with Miss King. Willy also said that I should not worry about George, that he is now in a very good situation. I am perplexed. Why does Willy think I have been worried about George? Or rather, *how* does he know? Did they meet, finally? Did George mention that I had written to him? I am afraid my brother will not be happy with what I have been up to. His letter was rather circumspect and much shorter than usual. I am certain that he is in low spirits. Or terribly angry with me.

Fitzwilliam Darcy

A cosmic event with celestial consequences HAS happened! Its name is Lady Catherine de Bourgh! I am jesting, but only a bit.

This afternoon, Aunt Catherine swept in with no prior notice, on her way, she said, from Longbourn back to Kent. I was astonished. What business did she have at Longbourn?

"My dear nephew, you are still young and may not be aware of the turpitude of the scheming world surrounding you," she began, in her patronizing way. "I have it on good authority, through my parson, Mr. Collins, that there have been rumors of an engagement between Miss Elizabeth Bennet and, can you guess whom?" She peered at me closely.

Elizabeth engaged! Could it be the Colonel? I felt the blood drain from my face but endeavored to remain nonchalant. "Please enlighten me, Aunt?"

"Well, be advised that some malicious gossip has fixed you, yes you, Fitzwilliam Darcy, as the lucky object of her schemes."

"Me?"

"Pray contradict this hideous falsehood and relieve my anxieties, although I know it to be quite impossible. It is, of course, quite impossible!" She continued looking at me narrowly with her anxious, angry beady eyes, which belied her certain knowledge of the impossibility of the fact. "You are not engaged to her?"

"No, I certainly am not!" I stated shortly.

She sighed in triumph and produced an ugly, crooked smile. "I see we are of one mind. You, like me, are shocked. You feel the abomination of this. As your parents are no longer there to help you navigate through the shoals of life, I felt it incumbent upon me to visit the lady in question as soon as I heard this rumor. You will be appalled at the rudeness and ill treatment I received from her."

"Miss Bennet was rude to you?" I asked, incredulous. "What was the nature of your conversation?"

"Oh, I had to hear from the mouth of that upstart, pretentious girl that she and you had formed no attachment. I had to hear this scandalous falsehood universally repudiated. I had to hear her promise that she would NEVER enter into any sort of engagement with you. And do you know what she did? Do you know she steadfastly opposed all my arguments against this unthinkable match? She, yes, that penniless girl, whose sister, barely fifteen! eloped with an officer, you know? Scandalous, vulgar family! You are stricken, speechless. I cannot blame you. But let me tell you what she said."

Lady de Bourgh took a slow turn about the room, breathing heavily, and it struck me that she was enjoying the theatrics of her revelations. I acted appropriately shocked and waited for her to continue.

"She claimed that if you felt so inclined and were to make an offer to her, it was of concern to nobody else. She said if you were to find happiness with her, and she with you, that was only between the two of you! Oh, I have never heard such impudence! After the condescension I showed her last spring! Ungrateful wretch! She said she would act only in the way that would determine her own happiness! That if she were your choice, why should she not accept you? And when I pointed out to her that she would be shunned by every good family, do you know what she replied?"

"I can't imagine."

"She said that the opprobrium of society at large would mean nothing to the wife of Mr. Darcy, who would necessarily find such extraordinary sources of happiness attached to her situation…"

"Are you quite sure she said that?" I asked, my heart beating faster with every syllable of the lady's inflamed speech.

"Oh yes, quite sure! I see you are as appalled as I am, and I confess I am relieved to see that her wily schemes have failed! Her frankness and directness were not to be borne! Little adventuress! She put on quite an air, she was quite serious and emotional. Acted as though she would make a fine match for you. Can you believe the audacity? Insufferable! I was never so insulted. She quite chased me off their miserable little property, you know! She accused *me* of insulting *her*! Can you conceive of greater impudence?"

I had trouble repressing a smile. "How odious," I murmured. I could just imagine the scene.

Lady Catherine raged on while tea was brought in, and the storm continued after the tea things were removed. She spared no detail. She was almost suffocating with spite, yet everything she related now made my heart sing. I was quite the actor, listening as if in shock, soothing her wrath with noncommittal monosyllables now and then, cleverly fishing for more details.

But oh, what joy! Once again, my aunt has unwittingly been the instrument of the heavens, sent down to give me my answer as to Elizabeth's feelings toward me. Had she really disliked me, I know that she would not have hesitated to tell Lady Catherine that she had no intention of allying herself with an arrogant, conceited, selfish man. She would have laughed in her face at the idea of such a marriage. No, instead she was "quite serious…emotional," and she stated that Mr. Darcy's wife "would have extraordinary sources of happiness…" From her frank responses to my bullying aunt, I knew that I could at least dare to hope.

While my aunt rambled on, I was trying to devise a way to get rid of her as soon as possible. I wanted to depart for Netherfield immediately and make a proper proposal to the woman I love. Luckily, Aunt Catherine did not want to tarry after having spent so much energy heaping this torrent of abuse on Elizabeth. She declared herself eager to return to Rosings, the carriage was ordered, and the lady left.

Tomorrow, at first light, I shall be on the road to Hertfordshire.

Fitzwilliam Darcy

Netherfield, October 6

I know it is a hackneyed phrase to talk about being the happiest of men or the happiest of couples, but I am that, and we are that. Well, that turn of phrase was rather incoherent, and although right now I have no *need* to confide to paper the turbulence of my thoughts, I *want* to confide my joy out of a sense of fairness. Let not just the unhappy times be recorded, but also the happy ones. I would like to get right to the point and declare, "SHE LOVES ME!" in capital letters, and be done with the business of writing and start with the business of living, but I owe it to this journal, which sustained me in times of trouble, to confide to it in my times of bliss.

Although my aunt's visit had quite convinced me of the fact that Miss Eliza did not implacably hate me, still, when the time came to visit Longbourn, I faltered a bit upon being the recipient of Mrs. Bennet's jaundiced glances. She is, however, so exultant in her eldest having made a good match that her attitude is somehow softened toward me. And keeping in mind that she is just a less wealthy version of my rather impolite aunt, I steeled myself to ignore any disagreeable look or speech. I had made up my mind yesterday that today would see either the culmination of my ardent desires or the sad ending of something that simply was not meant to be. I had to remove the torture of doubt.

I needn't have worried so much about Mrs. Bennet; no sooner had we exchanged the usual civilities than Charles, dear soul, had us immediately take to the lanes. A good breeze was bending the tall grasses and waving through the golden leaves on the trees. Charles and Jane swiftly managed to outpace us, while I was left with Kitty and Elizabeth. As soon as Kitty left us to go visit the Lucases, I grappled with how best to begin. My last attempt had not been felicitous, and so many thoughts crowded upon my brain that for a minute I was at a loss. But here Eliza saved me by embarking upon a speech that truly surprised me.

She said she knew that it was I who had found Lydia and brought her and George to matrimony, and she thanked me heartily, though with some embarrassment, for bringing it all about. She added that her family had no knowledge of what had occurred in London, but she wanted to thank me in their name. Here was my opening. After exclaiming that I never wished her to know any of what had happened, I stated that in doing what I did for her sister, I had thought only of *her*.

She was deathly quiet for a few seconds. I stole a glance down at her face. Her cheeks were flushed. She did not look angry, though. I had to continue. I risked it all. I could no longer bear the uncertainty. I put my pride at her feet and asked her if her feelings toward me were the same as they were last April.

"*My* affections and wishes are unchanged, but one word from you will silence me on this subject forever."

She halted abruptly. I stopped and turned to face her. The wind was whipping her bonnet strings in her face. Suddenly, she pulled at the strings and yanked off her bonnet, which gave me a clear and perfect view of her ever so fine eyes. I came a step closer. "Mr. Darcy," she said, looking up at me, but not so boldly as she had been wont to do in the past, and then glancing down again, "my feelings…my feelings are not, not at all, the same. At one point they were, but not anymore, I mean, not as they once were. They have taken quite a material turn. A turn that is so substantial, so complete, that I think that you…that is… I feel, what I feel is that…quite the reverse!" She stopped, aware of her rambling.

I was looking at her marvelous chestnut curls waving wildly and framing her sun-kissed face. Her words, though scattered, were like warm honey to my soul. I understood perfectly what she was trying to say.

She took a deep breath, seemingly rallying her courage and her wits, and looked at me with a smile. "Mr. Darcy. Forgive my dilapidated discourse. I am, I own, astonished that your feelings are unchanged. That your wishes and affections are unchanged. I am astonished, but happy. Happier than you might believe. For *my* feelings *have* changed. I was quite mistaken and confused for the longest time. But now it is certain that my affections rest with *you*."

I think I broke into what Georgiana calls my huge crocodile smile. I took her hand. She held mine and covered it with her other hand. The bonnet fell to the ground and we ignored it. Good Lord, the cosmic events were firing away! Aunt Catherine would probably have died of apoplexy to see us thus. "You are not displeased with my assurances that I admire and love you still, and that I still, and more than ever, wish you to be my wife?" I asked.

She laughed softly. "No, not displeased at all. Very pleased, indeed. It seems your wishes coincide quite neatly with mine."

Her bonnet now blew away under a heavier gust and went tumbling down the lane in a swirling jumble of autumn leaves. We ran to retrieve it. A woman who runs…and is very pretty. Yes, absolutely perfect, Georgiana had said. And now, at last, that woman was mine!

"I can hardly believe it," I said, as we resumed a more proper walking pace. "For a year, I have loved you heart and soul. You have no idea how many nights I have not slept, seeing your bewitching eyes before me. You are the dearest thing in my heart. I am not sure I would have ever recovered if you had told me just now that you felt no affection for me."

"Mr. Darcy, I had not the slightest idea…you are a great concealer! But you have been a generous soul throughout. Your feelings have been fixed like the North star, while I have been a fool, presuming to know all, judging all, mocking all, but only deceiving myself. I understood nothing, I dismissed what was important and built up inconsequential things. What you said about my family—"

"Abominations. Please forget what I said."

"But you were not in the wrong. To wit, my sister eloping with…a person you have every right to revile and condemn."

"No!" I said, perhaps too forcefully. "No. I must tell you… I may have been wrong. It has come to light that George Wickham is not as villainous as I once thought."

"But…what you wrote…about your sister…?" she said with a questioning frown.

"It is possible that an elopement was not in fact what George Wickham was after when he met my sister at Ramsgate."

"Now you have confused me thoroughly."

"There are some details that still escape me, and until I have understood it all, I think it best to think of Wickham in a better light. That is what I decided in London, when I saw how determined he was to do his duty by Lydia. And another thing I must tell you is that they were in fact married almost immediately upon reaching London, by a French priest. Not a proper Anglican wedding, to be sure, but two witnesses attested to it. So, it turns out your sister was not as flighty, and he not as morally corrupt, as we might have thought."

"Oh, that does put it in another light altogether! Poor Lydia is perhaps not so bad after all. But still, he took advantage of her unguarded manner and youth! That is eminently reprehensible! And what of his profligacy even before…?"

"Again, I must beg you to defer judgment even in these respects. There seems to have been only a small portion of responsibility on George

Wickham's account. I cannot tell you the details yet, but I ask you to trust me on this."

"Very well. George Wickham is henceforth not a villain. We have all been deceived one way or another, it seems! But are you sure you are not telling me this to assuage my sisterly sensibilities?" she asked.

"I assure you it is the truth as I believe it to be. I would not knowingly lie to you," I said. (Although there were some things I would not actually tell her just yet…) We were silent for a moment.

"So, perhaps Jane was right…" she mused out loud.

"In what respect?"

"When Mr. Wickham first told me of his misfortunes at your hands, I related these to Jane. She would not believe that you were such a blackguard."

"I have always liked your sister Jane!" I said, immediately regretting it, after all that I had done to ruin Jane's happiness. But Elizabeth did not take notice.

"She said it had to be a great misunderstanding, because Mr. Wickham seemed so truthful and gentle, and you were so honorable. She has such a loving heart, she can't believe there is wickedness in the world."

"Perhaps in this matter a loving heart is the best guide, and she was more in the right than you or I."

"I think she was. You know, Mr. Darcy, after Lydia's marriage to Wickham, I was convinced I would never see you again, because of the pain it would cause you to be reminded of this man's existence. It made me dreadfully despondent. So, when you returned to Netherfield with Mr. Bingley and came to visit us at Longbourn, I was quite taken aback. But I was hopeful that we might renew our friendship."

"I came back to see *you*. Wickham or no Wickham, I still would have come back."

"But why were you so silent during your visits?"

"I modeled my behavior on yours! You were guarded and taciturn, which you must admit is not your usual deportment!"

"I was afraid of your displeasure. I had no idea you had saved Lydia until she revealed it herself to me in a moment of thoughtlessness. She said it was supposed to be a big secret and you would be angry that she had let it out. I did not know how to broach the subject with you. Oh, Mr. Darcy, we are quite irrational creatures. How much simpler would life be if we just asked people pointblank what was on their mind?"

"Perhaps in some cases it would be simpler. In other cases, it might be insufferable. You recall of course that my aunt's philosophy is utter frankness and relentless interrogation."

She laughed. "Ah yes. Lady Catherine. You may not believe this, but she came to see me!"

"I know all about it. She came to my house in London directly from Longbourn to give me every detail of your impertinent ripostes to all her demands, accusations, and insults."

"Oh dear. I am afraid she did make me lose my temper."

"But if it weren't for her, I would never have had the audacity to hope."

"What do you mean?"

"I did not have enough confidence that your resentment against me had been extinguished. You do not know the tortures I endured. And then, this happened. Lady Catherine said you steadfastly refused to promise never to enter into an engagement with me. Tell me if this is true: she said that you stated that the wife of Mr. Darcy would have extraordinary sources of happiness."

"I did say something to that effect. She has been a faithful reporter."

"It cleared the doubts I was harboring. I knew that if you truly hated me you would have told her so directly."

"Yes, you know enough of my character to know of my frankness and abominable rudeness! But I had already effected that turn, that substantial change of direction of feelings. However, I had no reason to think my words would be repeated to you, or have any effect if they were. What folly to think you would not detest me! How could I hope that you would make an offer to me again, after the hideous rejection I subjected you to?"

"Your rejection was the perfect response to a hideous proposal. I deserved every reproof." I went on to explain how relentlessly my conscience tortured me with a rehearsal of every accusation and insult I had thrown upon her and her family. But she seemed anxious to forget the entire episode. I like the fact that she is turned toward the future. Pain that is past should be left in the past.

We talked on and on, discussing my letter, her change of heart, her recollections of what Wickham had said and done, while I did my best to reframe any perceived fault on his part to lessen his burden without telling her the entire truth. She seemed a little dubious, unsurprisingly, but seemed to acquiesce to the excuses I put forth.

The sun was red, sinking behind the trees, when we realized at last that we had been gone far too long. What would the Bennets think? She knew, of course, a shortcut through the woods. I held her hand as we jumped over ferns, I lifted her effortlessly across a shallow brook, and we ran back along a secluded path, laughing like children.

I will not write down what we did when we paused just before emerging from the woods, after we both had to stop, exhausted from our sprint. She rested her back against a huge oak tree and I am quite certain she beckoned me to come closer. All I can say is that I *think* she liked it very well, I *know* I liked it more than anything, and it only took a minute, or two.

"Well, Mr. Darcy, I am glad we are friends again," she said. I bowed, she curtsied. We laughed again.

She rearranged her bonnet, and we walked at a much slower pace back to the house, where the company was awaiting us for supper. Eliza convincingly described the imaginary pastoral scenes that had captured our attention for so long out of doors, while Bingley and even Jane smiled mischievously.

I am happy to have a woman who is very pretty and who likes to run, to share with me the rest of my life. I am the happiest of men.

Georgiana Darcy

On the heels of the amazing piece of news that I received from my brother yesterday, announcing his engagement to Miss Eliza Bennet (finally! a SISTER! this time she said YES!), today I received a long letter from Anne that escaped the censorship of her mother. What a difference from her usual platitudes! She says she has found a way to send letters privately, thanks to their new French cook who has taken her under her wing. I am eager to receive more missives from her like the following:

"Mr. and Mrs. Collins had a private audience with my mother yesterday, and being the dutiful daughter, I eavesdropped with great art while Mrs. Jenkins lay in a stupor. (She loves a little port after dinner and cannot remain awake after that!) I learned things that I found excessively diverting, and if I can truly in the future (merci, Madame Blanchard!) receive letters from you unintercepted by my mother, I would love your honest opinion on this. To make a long story a bit shorter—well, you do not personally know this Mr. Collins, our parson, but he is the most insufferable *man I have ever known, and every speech of his is either an obsequious disquisition or an apology—well, this Mr. Collins is married to a lady who was a neighbor and very good friend of Miss Elizabeth Bennet. I think I told you Miss Eliza came to visit Mrs. Collins in the spring and was frequently invited at Rosings. Well, Mr. Collins learned from his wife, whose mother wrote this news to her, that there was a great scandal in the Bennet family. The youngest girl eloped! Ran away! with the son of YOUR FORMER STEWARD, you know him very well, of course, George Wickham! They fled together and lived together, UNMARRIED, for weeks before they were discovered in London hiding in a hovel, and they were made to marry by the girl's uncle. Can you believe it? The girl is young, 14 or 15. I wonder that George would do such a thing; but then I have only childhood memories to go by. I remember him as being very kind to us, and very amusing, when I came to visit you at Pemberley when you were still very little. I think*

you liked him very well too. Isn't that the strangest thing? And it is unbelievable to me, because I came to know Miss Eliza and she seemed extremely well-mannered; it is hard to conceive that her sister would do something so untoward. Well, what a clamor of voices as Mr. and Mrs. Collins spread the news! My mother exclaimed, and Mr. Collins pontificated and rejoiced at his escaping being more closely related to that family than he already is. (He and Miss Eliza are cousins, and he had made an offer to her—which she refused.) Mrs. Collins was frequently relied on by my mother to give descriptions of the girls in the Bennet family after Miss Eliza's departure, so I feel that I almost know them. Mr. Collins finally requested my mother's permission to go visit the Bennets and "bestow upon them the balm of his pity and the censure of Her Ladyship's displeasure, with admonitions to the sisters against following in so wild a path," etc. With her blessing, he went. I think he is an ass, and I can just imagine how Miss Eliza will receive his pity and admonitions. She is witty and funny and not one to be harassed by imbeciles. Ah, well, and THAT is about the most exciting thing that has happened in a twelvemonth, and it hasn't even happened to me. I wonder what it would be like to escape with an officer. I giggle thinking about what my mother would say. But that, of course, will never happen. My mother refuses to let me leave Rosings, so Mr. Darcy's invitation to me to visit you at Pemberley has already been refused, I believe. She thinks I will immediately catch the plague and die. I do hope you can come visit."

Quite an interesting lot, those Bennet girls, indeed!

London, October 15

"Well, Georgiana, it appears you were quite busy writing and receiving letters all of last summer, which you had no business doing."

That is how the uncomfortable discussion I had been dreading for months began. I was unable to speak, and so I just stared at Willy, probably looking very foolish.

Willy had just returned from Hertfordshire. We were in the drawing room, alone, for once.

He smiled and continued: "Did you and George in fact correspond for several months?"

My mouth went very dry. I must have looked quite frightened.

"Do not be alarmed. I shall not scold you. But we do need to talk about George. You wrote to him?"

"I did write to him. I had to. Now that he is married to Eliza's sister, I can tell you everything."

So I did. How George had first corresponded with me through Mrs. Younge two years ago, telling me he had revelations about my family that were very important. How we planned a meeting at Ramsgate. How we were interrupted by Willy's arrival. How I was so flustered and still ignorant of what exactly George was going to tell me that I was incoherent, and my silly babbling led Willy to misunderstand the nature of the meeting. How a year later, I received that letter from George telling me to meet him by the brook. My ingenious strategies to correspond with him, which frankly led to nothing. I left out my attempt to flee Pemberley. No need to go into that failed and foolish idea!

"That was very deceitful of you, Georgiana." The words might have alarmed me, but he was still smiling kindly. It made it easier for me to be brave.

"I know, and I hated lying. But what can one do when one is powerless and has no other choice? At that time, I was convinced you were so disgusted with what I had done in Ramsgate that you would never listen to me rationally. And I feared for George's well-being. I was torn. Loyalty to you, or compassion for George? I tried to do both. An arduous task."

"I should have been more accessible to you, Georgiana. I am sorry. So, he told you the truth last summer. So you've known much longer than I have that our father was also George's father."

I looked at him and was surprised to see no bitterness or anger in his eyes, none of that armor glazing his soft brown eyes. "Yes. Not only from what George said, but from—well, I might as well admit that one day I eavesdropped—unintentionally, I assure you—on Mrs. Prescott and Mrs. Annesley. They were talking about their suspicions that George was not the son of Mr. Wickham. Willy, I understand many things, but I do not understand *why* our father… How could he…? It makes me sad. And what about Mrs. Wickham? Was she a victim or a willing um…consort? Was there love? And our mother? Did she know? Oh, I have so many questions, but I cannot imagine that you have the answers to them."

"I don't understand any of it either. And I suppose I should try to be wise and say it is not our place to understand. All I know is that our father was a good man, a respected man, a good father; our mother was a kind and loving mother. And that will not change. I hope you are not shocked."

I smiled. "No. Sad, yes, but not shocked. I have read novels where all sorts of strange things happen in families."

Willy rolled his eyes and smiled. "Ah, novels. Thank God for novels."

"Don't mock them. I would not be half so wise without them," I said jestingly. "But, my dear brother, I am so glad that thanks to *my* wise advice, all turned out well for you and Lizzie."

He laughed. "Indeed. I am grateful for your advice. And now between the two of you, I have little chance of going astray."

So, there we were, the wise older brother, the wise younger sister, both a little bewildered by what our parents had been up to. I felt that there was no chance of ever solving any of these riddles.

A date has been set for the wedding, and before the year is out, Pemberley will have a real mistress. I am overjoyed. I will show her all the wonderful places in the woods. There are a few abandoned cottages that I simply must look into, but Mrs. Annesley refuses to let me enter them, pretexting excessive dust and dirt. But I am curious. I am certain Elizabeth will agree to accompany me. She has a romantic turn of mind, like me, and what Gothic treasures shall we discover! We will have such fun. We will talk about novels. We will play and sing duets. I can go to her for advice about what to wear, and I can hardly wait for that! Mrs. Annesley has truly hideous taste when it comes to fashion.

Fitzwilliam Darcy

Pemberley, February 10

Lizzie and Georgiana get on so well, I am almost jealous! They have embarked on a project to revive and redecorate the old hunting lodge. It is situated about three miles from the house, in a deep part of the park that is seldom frequented. I am not sure which of my two fair ones is most excited about this endeavor. They walk there and then stay hours on end with a couple of domestics, sorting things and moving furniture, and I usually do not see them again until tea.

I miss them when they are out. My demons come to haunt me. I still cannot reconcile what I know of my father with the narrative of George's birth. I am still tortured by uncertainty. Did my father force himself on a woman who could not refuse him due to her subaltern position? Did she entrap him? Was he a scoundrel? Was my father unhappy with my mother? Did she drive him to this, or was she a miserable victim? I try to recall my parents' comportment with each other…but of course, we are English. Guarded and quiet. I had too few memories, too few clues.

One evening, about a month after our wedding, Lizzie asked me what was on my mind as she caught me once again staring at the portraits in the family gallery. I finally told her the entire history, the revelations of Mrs. Younge. I told her of my torment in not knowing whether my father was a scoundrel or an honorable man. She was surprised by the narrative but not shocked. "It is not for us to judge anyone in this regard," she said. "We simply do not know enough of what may really have happened. Remember that for almost a year I thought of you as an arrogant, selfish, prideful man. I thought I had all the facts at my disposal and that my powers of observation were unsurpassed. And I was completely in the wrong."

"Absolutely completely?" I asked with a smile.

"As absolutely completely as possible. We will never know all there is to know about other persons. So, forgive and forget. And remember my philosophy, we must remember of the past only what gives us pleasure."

"It is a sound philosophy. And your sister Jane's too—about not finding fault with anyone if at all possible."

"In the case of your father, I believe Jane's philosophy is to be followed. However strange people's behaviors may seem to us, let all parties be blameless!" she said playfully.

Our conversation helped relieve my mind. I hope Georgiana is not as afflicted as I am by these things. I think not. She seems very happy now that Eliza is here. I am grateful.

Gulliver

Pemberley, February 18

Today I accompanied Miss Georgie and Miss Lizzie to the hunting lodge. Humphrey came too, carrying parcels and brooms. They sure were lucky to have me along, because I smelled something as soon as we came into the lodge. In the back room there was a horrible, huge beast. A rat. I smelled it long before Miss Georgie saw it. But when I dislodged it and it went scampering, she screeched. I chased it well into a rotting piece of woodwork. The battle was fierce. Humphrey came with his broom. A rickety old table was turned over, and dusty volumes and papers flew and scattered onto the floor. I heroically caught the beast and slew it. I am proud to say that he is no longer of this world. What a gross animal. That tail is vile. But what an epic scene!

After all the screaming, Miss Lizzie rallied forth. She directed Humphrey to pick up the nasty bloodied quivering corpse, and she and Miss Georgie, coughing with all the dust, started picking up the things. Nobody congratulated me, which I find extremely odd. I hope they will tell Master Willy that I saved the day. I settled myself for a nap, but they roused me and we left in a big hurry.

Fitzwilliam Darcy

Pemberley, February 18

Today my ladies returned much earlier than expected. I heard them from the library and went out to meet them. In the hall, Lizzie whispered something to Georgiana, who hurried up the stairs. Lizzie came toward me with a serious countenance.

"Willy," she said, "Georgiana and I have done something wicked."

"I am delighted. I expect a full confession," I said flippantly. I am getting used to Lizzie's playacting.

But her eyes were brimming with tears, and I realized her seriousness was not feigned.

"We came upon some writings in the lodge, and before we realized what it was, we had read too far…something that should perhaps have remained private. But I believe *you* should read it."

I instantly became serious too. Lizzie is not a weeping willow, so this had to be important. She handed over a sheaf of papers. I recognized my father's penmanship in the title written on the top page.

Judge Not, That Ye Be Not Judged

"I believe your father wrote this, and we started reading it, thinking it might be an amusing anecdote… We read too far into it… I am very sorry. We did not realize. We had no right, really. Shall I leave you alone?"

"No. I have no secrets from you, Lizzie. You say my father wrote this? How do you know? You cannot know his handwriting."

"I glanced at the end, his signature is there. It looks like…like a confession of sorts."

"Please have Georgiana summoned. I do not wish to harbor secrets from either of you. There have been too many secrets. I abhor them, for they almost ruined my chance of happiness with you."

When Georgiana arrived, we all three went to sit by the fireplace. My wife and my sister sat next to each other, and I facing them. I decided I would read it aloud. If my father had written a confession, whatever it might be, I wanted my family to hear it all.

I have come back to this place again to do justice to my own memory, and to that of Eleanor, and that of Alan.

I do not write this to exonerate myself but for the peace of my own mind. As I am getting older, and my wife has passed from this world, the memories return and haunt me. I must couch the truth on paper. In the meanders of my mind, it is too troublesome to keep all this. Let this parchment hold my confession, let it carry my burden, and let it contain a testament to my happiness.

It all happened innocently. Of course, we knew it was not within the realm of propriety. In the eyes of God, and society, perchance it was a sin. But what portion of that sin was brought about by loyalty, what portion by love, what portion by the horrors of war? What is certain is that malice had no part in this history.

The extraordinary request I received from my old friend Alan at first filled me with dread. And yet to this request I owe the recollections that still set my heart beating like that of a young man, though all my friends have passed, and I know my time grows short.

First, I must sum up my debt to Alan Wickham.

As the third son, I had chosen to be a hero abroad. Better to be gallantly fighting the French in America, thought I, little knowing what a hideous thing war was, than to live an idle life as the idle youngest brother of a couple of idler still young men who existed for pleasure and society.

I was quickly undeceived as to the glory of soldiering. Bitter cold, discomfort, disease. Not a moment of privacy. Reprimands, floggings, food shortages, executions. All that is horrid in our world contained and multiplied in the military life. Yet not all was bad. Friendships were formed in the bosom of hardship, and when I found out that Alan Wickham hailed from Derbyshire, we formed a fast companionship. I talked of my brothers. He talked of his sweetheart, who had pledged to wait for his return, a promise of which he was not so sure because she had a rare beauty and would easily find suitors in his absence.

In the frigid territories of Canada, nary a soul was left unmoved by the beauty of this virgin land, its immense forests and magnificent rivers, and Alan often remarked it would not be the worst fate to stay here in the New World, eventually. But it was a cruel land too. And we were not there to admire the views.

At the Anse-au-Foulon, after a dreadful siege of three months during which half the soldiers were lying desperately ill, many succumbing amidst the most horrible suffering, those of us who were still healthy were finally summoned to battle. As we were engaging the French garrison at Quebec, when it seemed we would be victorious, I was struck in the ankle, and then in the elbow. I fell, wild with pain and shock, knowing death was coming as I saw a crazed-looking enemy aiming now at my chest.

My comrade-at-arms Alan interposed his body, shooting the Frenchman dead but in the process receiving the enemy's musket ball in the abdomen. His cry of agony as he fell, I will never forget. We both lay there groaning for hours, falling in and out of consciousness, supporting each other as best we could with words of encouragement and reciting prayers. With my good arm I tried to stanch the flow from Alan's wound. I was unable to do anything. My own blood seemed to be seeping out forever, mingling with his in a horrific puddle.

I was certain Alan would die, as the loss of such a quantity of blood seemed too injurious to survive. I tried to crawl away to seek help, but he begged me not to leave him. I was convinced then that we would both die, along with many others whose rasps tore the air. But, miraculously, by the grace of God, we were picked up at last and removed from the nauseating stench of blood and gore on what they call the Plains of Abraham. We were nursed back to health, which was a miracle in Alan's case, as his wound was a hideous one from which only the strongest constitution could have survived.

We learned that England had been victorious, though we lost our general, but Alan and I were no longer fit to serve (thank God!) and were repatriated within a twelvemonth.

What a change at Pemberley when I hobbled back, expecting a hero's welcome and finding only desolation and more death! My two elder brothers, neither of them married, had succumbed to the influenza, leaving the estate impoverished by their profligacy. I was the sole heir, and for weeks, in a daze, I limped and paced through the great halls that were still creped for my brothers.

A marriage was arranged by my aunt, with a lady a little past her prime. Lady Anne was a quiet woman, a little low in spirits but of a wealthy family, and I dared not oppose the match. I had sad prospects. Who would want a limping man with only one good arm? And she would resurrect the estate with her considerable dowry. We were married within six months of my return to England.

About two years after my marriage, Alan came to visit me with his charming young wife. The sweetheart had been true to her word. But Alan was in rather desperate pecuniary circumstances. I offered him the management of Pemberley, which he readily and gratefully accepted.

Now comes the part where shame and glory still dispute the greater share in my heart. Still a few years later, when after several stillbirths, we had finally had a fine, healthy boy (Fitzwilliam was a happy lad just starting to crawl), one day, as Alan and I were examining trees that might need thinning in a distant part of the park, Alan explained, with some difficulty, that he could not perform [here I paused, wondering if I should continue, a little concerned that this might shock Georgiana, but I decided I needed to proceed] *...that he could not perform conjugal duties as a consequence of the blow he had received in battle. I was shocked. The memories of that awful year of illness, drudgery, and war came back in all their hideousness. That musket ball was meant for me, and he had risked his life to save mine. He did not bring that up, of course, as he was too loyal and humble to make any such remark. But Eleanor, his beloved wife, desperately wanted a child, he said. He did too. He asked me if I could help. He looked at me, his pale eyes unflinching, until I understood his meaning.*

As a man of honor, I could not accept, with regards to Anne, and I told him so. He said he understood, but went away looking defeated.

I resisted several months, until they came together to plead with me.

They were both acutely embarrassed, but she spoke firmly. "We shall ask nothing of you, Sir, nothing more. You will not be burdened with anything regarding the child."

"Is there no other way...no other...person who could...?"

"We cannot count on anyone else's discretion, Sir. Who would you have us go to? A ruffian, a farmer? They will talk. They will make demands. They will claim the child. You are our only hope."

Mrs. Wickham was a personable, charming woman, blonde and blue-eyed. I felt troubled, looking at her. I did not want to be unfaithful to Anne, even though I was under orders not to touch my wife for the rest of our lives after the three stillbirths and the difficult birth of Fitzwilliam. Yet flesh [here again I almost faltered...but perhaps novels had inured Georgiana to all the rigors of life, and she seemed unperturbed] *Yet flesh has its demands, and although I was not in the first bloom of youth, I was still vigorous. I was tempted. But I kept shaking my head. "I cannot. It is quite impossible."*

Mrs. Wickham started to weep. "You do not know what it is like, to be childless. Doomed to a bitter old age. Please. Is it such a sin? We will make sure nobody ever knows."

I felt my resolve waning. "Lady Anne must never suspect."

"She shan't."

"I don't want you to hate me, Alan. What if you resent this, later? This is not a game of cards. We have been friends a long time."

His pale eyes glistened. "That is why I asked you, William."

He had called me "Mr. Darcy" ever since he had become my steward. His renewed use of my Christian name brought me back to the encampment, our good times, our horrible times, our close touch with Death.

"Because we are friends," he continued. "Because you are honorable. It was my idea, but Eleanor and I have been discussing it for months, nay, over a year. I want a child as badly as she does. We beg you. I beg you. In the name of all that you and I went through, over there, on the Plains of Abraham."

It was arranged. Alan Wickham would travel to Scotland on some pretext several times for weeks on end, to make it less awkward. I entrusted Mr. and Mrs. Younge, a newlywed couple, very much in love, with a few particular arrangements. I knew these servants would never betray my secret, as I had been instrumental in their being able to marry and in providing them with situations at Pemberley. I told them nothing of the nature of the "agreement." What they thought of what happened in the hunting lodge, I do not know. They were very discreet and gave us ample berth. Eleanor would meet me there in the middle of the night, by prearrangement. The windows were hung with heavy draperies. I never really saw her, except by the faintest candlelight.

At first, I would stay only the time that it took. But then...then, later, we lingered. We talked. We laughed. Perhaps then it became a sin. The bonds of the flesh are cruelly imperious. They are too easily dismissed as vulgar by those who have never known this felicity. Although she was extremely shy in the beginning, Eleanor had none of the stiffness and taciturnity of Anne. And she, unlike Anne, was beautiful, young, healthy. Those nights were the happiest ones in my life. I had not foreseen the danger of falling in love. I had thought of myself as a sensible, rational, older man, crippled, past his prime. I felt like a young buck in her arms.

In a few months, Eleanor was with child, and my obligation over. Alan's journeys to Scotland ceased. He was ecstatic, thankful, unsuspecting of the happiness his wife had procured to me. I would see the couple sometimes walking in the lanes at Pemberley. I would feel proud, seeing her blooming with our baby. I was happy for them both, but resentful that our nights of passion were over, that Eleanor was not mine. This beautiful woman was carrying my child, and I would never be able to claim her, or the child, as mine.

When she died in childbed, I was as devastated as Alan was. I had a long talk with Alan. I promised I would do as much as I could to ensure that our little boy, Eleanor's little George, would lack for nothing. And I promised that

I would let nothing transpire of my role in his birth. No one would ever know. We did not want Eleanor's memory sullied. But I was sad and grief-stricken, and I was not allowed to mourn openly.

I think Anne started suspecting the truth. She caught me in unguarded moments. She never asked me anything about it, but eventually she insisted that we resume our life as husband and wife, despite the midwife's strict orders. She would summon me on certain days. And so, I would leave my chamber to meet her in hers, but rarely and dispassionately. Sometimes, she would come to me. In the ten years that ensued, she was with child several times, but could not carry any to term, until at last little Georgiana made her way into the world. The birth was long and difficult, again, and Anne never really recovered. Two years later, she was gone. Mrs. Prescott never uttered a reproach in my direction, but her accusing looks were eloquent enough.

I have devoted myself to making Pemberley what it once was, and I have succeeded, I think. I have great love for the people on the estate, and I try to ease their lot as much as possible. I have not enforced the enclosure laws, in fact, I disregard them entirely. And my tenants, I believe, return my affection. The estate is prosperous and beautiful. I have done my duty. Pemberley, its trees, its forests, its brooks, ponds, and waterfalls, its animals, these are also a testament to happiness. May they procure some joy to my sons and my daughter and, God willing, their descendants.

Perhaps someone will read this and know what I have done. But it shall not matter. Eleanor is gone, Alan is gone, Anne is gone; and soon life shall come to an end for me too. I am weary. I am left alone, thinking as much of my ghosts as I do of my living children. I watch my sons with a happiness tempered with fear that their likeness will be discovered. Fitzwilliam, strong, brilliant, and good-tempered, is the pride of my life, as sweet little Georgiana is my joy, but I found time to be alone with my beloved "godson" now and then. As a boy, he would listen with rapt attention as I told him of Alan's heroism, of the horrors of war, and of the beautiful and cruel wilderness of Canada. I never mentioned Eleanor.

I write this so that I may remember, when my time comes to depart, that I should not harbor any bitterness, for I did have a great share of happiness, when so many have none. And I bless that little hunting lodge.

William Darcy

Gulliver

March 10

Nice, nice, nice! Happy to have Miss Eliza around! It looks like she is staying a lot longer than last time. I take her on walks and runs every day, sometimes with Miss Georgie, sometimes without, sometimes with Master Willy, sometimes without, sometimes all three (my favorite times).

Yesterday was a "with Master Willy" afternoon. It was snowing, but that did not deter my humans. We took a long walk; we ran a little. Then we stopped in the hunting lodge. I love that place—the site of my rat-slaying triumph. It looks nice inside now, Miss Eliza and Miss Georgiana have made it comfortable.

The snow was falling hard. Master Willy made a roaring fire. It snowed all night. We stayed in the hunting lodge. Such a small bed for three, but I made myself comfortable on half of it, and they did not bother me.

And this morning, very early, when they let me out, I sank my paws into the softest, coldest snow. Marvelous! And then, I caught a crow! I really did. Just to teach the impudent fellow. But I didn't sink my teeth into his ridiculously small head, and I didn't want those nasty feathers in my throat. So I let him go.